CLAIMED BY THE MOBSTER

EVIE ROSE

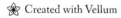

CONTENT NOTES

These content notes are made available so readers can inform themselves if they want to. They're based on movie classification notes. Some readers might consider these as 'spoilers'.

- Bad language: frequent
- Sex: fully described sex scenes with dirty talk
- Violence: on and off page
- Other: death of side characters, threat of death, dubious consent, kidnap, drugging, rough sex, age gap, ex-boyfriend's dad, breeding

1

ANWYN

Even though it's dark and pouring with rain, I hesitate before climbing the steps to the imposing London townhouse. With the orange glow of streetlights, shiny black tarmac, and low dark sky flickering around me, I run through my options again. I search desperately for a better alternative than throwing myself at the mercy of my ex-boyfriend's dad.

Cold water seeps between my toes and fogs my brain. Mr Crosse was always kind to me, in an offhand way. He's a bigger, grumpier, intimidating version of his son. Generous too, encouraging Tom to treat me with gifts and telling me I was welcome here anytime. He meant as Tom's guest, I suppose.

I'm testing that statement tonight.

Who else have I got who I can ask? I've walked miles across London and cannot afford pride. I mount the steps and press the bell, huddling a bit as a gust of wind tries to snatch my hood and succeeds in plastering it against my face. Ugh. December in London is miserable.

As the door opens, I ready the speech I prepared on the

walk over. All about how I know Mr Crosse—or rather his son Tom—and please would they let Mr Crosse know I'm here and why I need his charity in the form of a bed for the night.

"Miss Kendrick." Framed by the yellow light, Mr Crosse takes up the whole doorway and my throat goes dry. My lips are gummed together. The carefully crafted speech slices into my tongue.

He remembers me. Even as a drowned rat in a waterproof coat, he knows who I am?

My eyes take a second to adjust from him being a massive shadowed presence, to a man I've seen many times.

But none of them like this. I saw he was handsome before, but only in an abstract way. I didn't *want* him. My core didn't tingle. Somehow I missed Mr Crosse's raw sexuality.

He's dressed in a dove grey shirt undone at the neck and rolled to the elbows, revealing muscled forearms with a dusting of black hair. But his face. I don't know how aggressively masculine he is with his stubble, hard jawline, and severe nose. How did I ever breathe when he was around? I guess he was just my boyfriend's dad.

But he's not anymore.

He stands back, silently inviting me inside. I follow him into the house. I haven't been here for two years, since Tom and I left school and went to university. He broke up with me in our first term apart. We're still friends. We were just friends, really. Never even kissed properly. I tried, but Tom only hugged me and gave a peck of a kiss. I think he liked the symbol of a girlfriend and the reality of a friend.

The Crosse house is just as understated traditional luxury as I remember. Thick wallpaper in creams and blues, with intricate patterns of leaves, flowers and birds.

And I'm standing here, in my cheap waterproof and yoga pants that are soaked over the thighs.

Kill me now.

"Sorry." I shrink back, dripping on the front mat.

Mr Crosse takes me in, a sweeping look from my soaking canvas shoes to my hood, covering the strands of beige hair that worked out of the ponytail as I walked.

"Tom's not here."

"I know," I whisper miserably. I would have texted him if he was, but we've sort of lost touch recently. He's always too busy to talk to me now.

I meet Mr Crosse's gaze, expecting to find distaste in the grey eyes he gave to Tom, but no. It's not that. Just a curiously intense expression.

I'm shedding water everywhere. I shouldn't have come, it was a humiliating mistake. "I'll go—"

"Best get you out of those wet clothes," he interrupts as he reaches out and draws down the zip of my waterproof.

My breath clogs in my throat.

It's nothing. Only him undoing my coat, but I'm peeled like a banana. Exposed and my cheeks heating, as he grasps the lapel and slowly lifts it.

He hasn't touched me. He's totally respectful and appropriate as he helps me out of the soaked garment. He's not interested in a girl half his age with no experience, who used to date his son. It's me who is being weird. My body is bubbly all of a sudden. I'm a bottle of fizzy pop that has been sitting on the shelf, inert and dull, then seeing Mr Crosse has unscrewed the cap. There's sensation everywhere. Little crackles as Mr Crosse's eyes glide over me, bursts of awareness of my clothes on my skin.

Wet yoga pants are not erotic. They aren't. Just objectively. But my pussy is defying that law of physics and is heating as Mr Crosse eases my coat from my shoulders. The bedraggled garment is hung up while I watch, so confused and turned on, I can't bring myself to say or do anything but press my thighs together.

"Come." He turns and strides away and I'm left trotting to catch up. We twist through the house to a room I've never been in. It's a cosy library and I barely repress a gasp. The walls are covered with dark wood bookshelves and a table has old maps unfolded. Flames flicker in a large fireplace and two plush chairs are placed on either side. Mr Crosse gestures to one chair and folds his massive body into the other, taking a glass of amber liquid from a side table and swirling it thoughtfully.

I sink into the seat and struggle to begin my explanation of why I've turned up at his house. But instead of a coherent story, what emerges is, "I need somewhere to stay for tonight."

Mr Crosse nods slowly, goes to take a sip of his drink. Whisky? But he stops as the glass touches his lips, lowering it again and swallowing hard. His hand encompasses that chunky glass—I bet it's crystal—like it's nothing. A toy. But I can see it would be solid if I lifted it.

What would it be like to be touched by his hands? So strong and big.

"Do you mind my asking what happened?" His voice is a calm rumble, and though he couched it as a question, it's not. It's a command.

I guess he's used to not having to ask twice.

Mr Crosse is a huge deal. Country girl that I am, I didn't know anything about the London mafias when I was going out with Tom, and when he told me his dad was the kingpin of Westminster, I scoffed. Ridiculous.

Not ridiculous, as it turns out. My mafia-obsessed

housemates have been swooning over Westminster, the most influential of the London mafias, as well as giggling about the Bratva. Even I've seen photos in the gossip magazines of mafia bosses. And if I looked a bit longer at the ones with Benedict Crosse in them... I'm only human, alright? A virgin, not a pot plant.

And if I had any options, I'd be literally anywhere else.

The truth is, he's still the only person I know in this city. I assumed a lifetime of being a scholarship student at a posh boarding school had prepared me for university, but it didn't.

I'm shy, I guess. I don't know how to make friends, and have no family. None alive who want me, anyway. My aunt and uncle were happy enough to ship me to boarding school and there was never a good time for me to see them, so I stayed there for holidays too. Until Tom asked me to be his girlfriend, and I finally had somewhere to go. I thought being in London would force me to be more outgoing, but it's all so expensive. I'm left working shifts at a coffee shop and falling into bed having done nothing but work and study.

"I have to get some sleep tonight. I'll lose my bursary if I don't."

He doesn't say anything and his excessive patience is in big black capital letters. MR CROSSE IS WAITING.

I curse myself. I had this all worked out logically, but seeing him has me out of whack. "I share a student house with five girls. It's in Whitechapel and it's really cheap."

Nope. Still not making any sense.

"Five. And currently, around forty of their closest friends and more bottles of vodka than I've ever seen in my life."

A huge Sunday night party I first heard about when the

music was turned up at eight. Two hours later, I was about ready to tear my hair out. I know by now that there's no point in asking them to keep it down.

"I tried to stop it, but..." No one in that house listens to me. When I switched the music off I got elbowed out of the way and shouted out of the room. I called the police, but they said they couldn't do anything.

Last night they had a massive party too, and if I'm not on my A-game tomorrow, I'll be kicked off my scholarship, and so the end of going to university. Two years of work and student loans wasted. That means I won't have my dream job of being a plant geneticist and I'll probably be working in the Lazy Bean coffee shop until I'm eighty.

You know, I should have gone with that. It would be better than Mr Crosse's look of polite confusion.

Or I could have opted for the slightly less apocalyptic choice of getting a hotel room. But I did that yesterday, and last Saturday, and payday isn't until next week. I'm more terrified of debt and failure than I am of severe Mr Crosse and the feelings he evokes in me.

I am.

Probably.

Scary mobster or not, I'm out of options.

"I have an exam tomorrow. If I don't get any sleep tonight, I'll definitely fail."

"Mmm," he says, a muscle twitching in his jaw. "I'll find you alternative accommodation."

"There's no need," I rush to assure him. I cannot afford to get a new place. The landlord will take my deposit and the whole year of rent, and I'm broke enough as it is. "I just have to have somewhere for tonight. The house is usually fine."

He stares me down. "Evidently not."

"Except for the parties," I concede. And that most of my housemates loathe me. But lalalala, let's ignore that since I can't do anything about it. The rent is super cheap.

He scowls and runs his fingers around the rim of his glass.

Lucky glass.

I lick my lips and remind myself that lusting after your ex's dad is not the behaviour of good girls who study hard and have successful careers studying plants.

Mr Crosse—Benedict Crosse the gossipy article said, and I obviously cannot allow myself to think of this gorgeous man as anything as intimate as just his first name—folds his arms over his chest and looks into the fire. He glances back at me and for a second I'm sure it's an admiring look, speculative, yes, but not in the "what am I going to do with her" way. More, "what wouldn't I like to do to her".

Then it's gone, and he unfurls himself, standing so much taller than me. He approaches and my mouth waters. He's big, and my head is level with his crotch. I could...

Stop it, Anwyn. He won't ever think of you like that. But my mind does a slideshow of smutty images anyway, blurry as they are since they're based on books rather than reality.

"I'll take you to your bedroom now. And in future, when your housemates are having a party, you come here."

2

BENEDICT

Six months later

I deserve torment.

Don't get me wrong, I have done many bad things in the pursuit of power and I'm sure I have a penthouse in hell waiting for me. Every violent and ruthless action I've ordered—I don't tend to get blood on my hands directly anymore, but obviously I used to—marks my soul as much as scars cover my body under this suit. I absolutely should burn for all the dark acts I've committed to keep my people safe and my mafia as the foremost in London.

But surely, *surely*, I do not deserve this.

I wait a moment before I look up as Anwyn hovers in the doorway to my office. I pretend I haven't given everyone strict orders that from Saturday afternoon to Sunday late morning I am not to be disturbed unless it is a crisis of the highest magnitude.

I feel her eyes on me and it's this bittersweetness. Anwyn is an angel. Far too young for me. Much too innocent. She's beautiful and funny and she's my son's ex-girlfriend.

"Hello." I push my keyboard away.

She smiles tentatively. "Hello, Mr Crosse."

"Benedict."

"I can't call you that." She shakes her head ruefully, as she has a dozen times before.

I wonder if she knows she ought to call me Mr Crosse to keep me at a distance. If she calls me my given name it might be too easy to forget all the reasons Anwyn is forbidden to me. Not just because of her youth and her relationship with my son. No, I was forcibly reminded recently that the other mafias will use anyone I care about to leverage the absolute power I hold over London.

No doubt Marco Brent figured out that I have a soft spot for Anwyn because he has a bride even younger. There's no such thing as too careful, so I've had to become more circumspect in my behaviour towards Anwyn.

But I want her.

From the tips of her honey-blonde hair to her pastel-varnished toes, I can never get enough. A glimpse of her peaches-and-cream skin, like today when she's wearing a short-sleeved T-shirt, and I'm overwhelmed with the desire to find the places where she's pink and sensitive, and make her feel good.

I suppose many people long for Saturday night as much as I do. I believe it's considered something of an opportunity to relax. But it's not relaxing when Anwyn is with me. She's a temptation like no other, as she's curled on the sofa in my office, reading. Not having her with me chips away at my soul, but her presence tests my patience. I thought my self-control was unbreakable until I saw her on the doorstep that night. Fucking egotistical. Every week I hold on by a thread, and manage not to ravage her. Wreck her.

My son's ex-girlfriend. When I told him about Anwyn coming over because her house is a noisy shit-hole, he thanked me. He sounded surprised, and said to tell her hi, and he'd see her when he was back for the holidays. I think I know the reason he loves her as a friend, but still. She is—or was—his girlfriend and best friend.

Students should have longer terms, the vacations are too damn long. Thankfully Tom had plans for nearly all of it, only staying for a few days between mountain climbing trips with his new friends.

"They started the party early today, huh?" I lean back into my office chair and take in the sight of Anwyn in the doorway. She has her hair down today, falling over the small rise of her breasts. There's a hint of anxiety in her blue eyes and she nibbles on the plush pink of her bottom lip.

It's only four o'clock. Anwyn's visits have crept forward, week by week.

"You don't mind, do you?" She doesn't meet my gaze, the whites of her eyes flashing like a wary animal.

I swallow, my throat dusty, and wave her in. "Of course not."

I love that I get longer with her, and I hate it. Having to control myself even longer is my favourite punishment.

"I brought some work to do while you finish up." She indicates her armful of books like they're tickets of admittance and I'll inspect them.

I did once. Amongst her textbooks about trees was a single paperback with a floral cover. Totally innocuous, and I'd have passed right over it.

But the way she snatched it back, cheeks bright red, and

muttered, *it's just a novel,* was not innocent. I looked up the title later, and suffice to say, it wasn't *just* anything.

My girl was reading pure unadulterated smut while sitting opposite me. The book had an older hero and a virgin heroine. Knowing she reads that really doesn't help the constant hard-on I have when she's around.

I'm my own worst enemy.

This whole, spending the afternoon together, thing was at my instigation. At first Anwyn arrived just before ten o'clock and went straight to bed. It was good to have her safe under my roof, but far from enough. I suggested hot chocolate, and we stood around in the kitchen drinking it. Soon we were sitting in the library for two hours, spinning out the tepid drinks while we talked. When she accepted biscuits eagerly, I enquired about whether she'd eaten.

Suffice to say I was furious to discover she'd only had a snack since lunchtime. I shouldn't have demanded she arrive in time for dinner the next week, it was a step too far. But she arrived at seven and a light casual pasta supper the first time turned into three courses with one glass of wine— only ever one—coffee and chocolates afterwards.

"More plant genetics?" I ask as she goes to her usual place—the leather sofa adjacent to my desk.

"Yeah." She opens a textbook onto her lap. No girl porn reading today, and I don't know if I'm relieved or disappointed. It's a warm evening and she's wearing a pair of cut-off denim shorts with a blue T-shirt that matches her eyes.

She's so adorable my palms itch.

I click my mouse around, pretending to work, as I covertly watch her. Having Anwyn here has the weird effect of relaxing me as well as putting my whole body on high alert. "How did your exam go?"

"I got ninety-two per cent." She says it cautiously, like

that might not be enough, but raises those blue eyes to mine to drown me. "Top of my class."

Never thought I'd be entranced by a girl half my age, and absolutely never imagined she'd be incredibly smart as well as beautiful.

"Good girl. I'm proud of how hard you worked for that."

She glows under my praise, shoulders lowering and wriggling into the sofa, kicking off her shoes and tucking her feet under her to get comfortable. "Thanks."

So pretty. I'd love her to snuggle into me like that.

I guess she sees me as a father figure, caring and asking about her work. I even scold her a little when she doesn't do well on a test because she didn't spend enough time studying. This dynamic we've fallen into is part Sugar Daddy, part friend, a smidge of mentor.

I enjoy all of that. I just wish we could add, *lover. Husband.*

The time before dinner was introduced by Anwyn, and it has crept up. She used to arrive just before food, letting herself in with the key I gave her. About two months ago I was firefighting a territory issue with Lambeth and couldn't leave my office. She tiptoed in, and I murmured that she should entertain herself while I finished up. And that's how we began to spend half of Saturday together.

She studies and I clear some emails for an hour—how mafia bosses still get emails I don't know. I should just shoot anyone who asks questions I've already answered, but I don't because Westminster has legitimate aspects to the business, pretending to be law-abiding. Can't murder people; we have to disappear them.

Deniable. Westminster is all about the veneer of respectability over absolute power and wealth. That's one of many reasons I cannot act on my desire for this young woman.

"Ready to eat?" I ask when a respectable amount of time has elapsed. Anwyn nods eagerly, and I have a sudden vision of her on her knees, eating something else. Taking my cock in her mouth. Heat flares and the thought is closely followed by the image of her on my desk, legs spread, my own personal buffet. I'd gorge myself on her.

What a fuck up. I'm rock-hard from the smallest fantasy of her.

She's your son's ex-girlfriend, you arsehole, I remind myself. The dignity of Westminster demands I keep my needs to myself, subtly hiding my erection as I stand.

My chef has excelled herself this evening, and I resolve to give her a raise when Anwyn falls on the aperitifs with a happy sigh and exclamations of how tasty the food is. Now we're officially not working, she chatters about her week when I prompt her. We eat and talk, and I allow myself to enjoy her company.

This is bad. Painful, in a literal sense because I have to keep my aching cock under the table and away from Anwyn's curious gaze, when what I really want is her touch.

But it's only the beginning of my suffering, I'm aware that the worst is yet to come.

Once she leaves in the morning, that's when the feeling of emptiness sets in. It'll be a whole week without her before she's under my roof again, giving me that shy smile, her caramel hair laid on her collarbones and her scent—roses—surrounding me.

It's once she's left to return to her student life, young and brimming with potential, that I'm stabbed with how alone I am. My son has turned his back on the mafia. There are my staff around me, but none of them see past the severe looks or the sharp suits. They don't *see* me. Not like she does. I'm utterly alone without her and it's agony for those hours until the scouring pain eases.

And every Sunday morning, like she's my fucking religion, it's the same worship. She says she'll go. I insist on her eating first. We have breakfast in the light-filled kitchen, sitting at the breakfast bar side by side. She talks a lot on Saturday nights, but during our Sunday mornings there's easy silence, with her stealing glances at me while she nibbles at the croissants and jam that are her favourite. I think it's comfortable for her, anyway. For me, it's a wrench, forcing myself not to spin out her company any longer. I repeat in my head she will never want me the way I crave her, and this has to be enough. It must be, because I cannot scare her away with the depth of my longing.

"I really have to go," she says once I've scowled at her for refusing a third pastry, and we've irrefutably finished our coffees.

"Have a good week." I don't say that I'm insane without her and I miss her when she's not here like she's my frontal lobe.

When George has phoned me on the return journey and confirmed that she's safe, I give in. I get into the shower, turn the heat to scalding, and jerk myself off to the fresh image of Anwyn.

I'm brutal with my poor aching dick, which doesn't know what it's done wrong and can't help but respond to her more than any other woman. It's bordering on pain, sharp and rough, when I spurt the evidence of my desire over the tiles.

Each week I wash it away and say I shouldn't do this

again. That I should send her to a hotel, or at least not make myself come with her name on my lips.

It's a lie. Just one more bad action I've taken. Desperately lusting after this slip of a girl, too perfect, young, and innocent for me.

My son's ex-girlfriend.

Fuck.

And the absolute worst thing?

There was a time, not so long ago, that I looked at her with utter indifference. I barely noticed her and I don't think Tom saw her as a woman either. When I gave Tom "the talk", he blushed furiously and confessed they'd never even kissed. Obviously I didn't point out to my closeted son that wasn't normal. I just told him I loved him and he could tell me anything.

I had forgotten all about Anwyn until she turned up that night.

A good man would wish that had never changed and I'd never opened my eyes six months ago and seen Anwyn. So sweet and ripe, I wanted her the same moment her eyes met mine. I was putty in her hands.

I am a bad man. Because I don't want to go back.

Sunday is typically awful, and I throw myself into work. As the sun sets, red and purple through the window, I stretch out my fingers and sigh. Six long days until I see her again.

I work late, then collapse into bed, mercifully too exhausted to do anything but drag covers over me and fall asleep in the coal-black darkness.

The shrill ring of my phone wakes me. Dread wipes away sleep instantly. My people don't call me in the middle of the night about nothing.

The screen shows my most-trusted lieutenant, my

second-in-command. He accompanied Anwyn home this morning, always does.

"She's in danger."

Adrenaline floods me.

"Why?" I snap. I don't ask who. We both know who. There is only one *she* who justifies waking me.

"We can't be sure. I just got a tip-off. A message came through the website for the shell company that sells garden furniture saying there was a hit out from the Bratva on Anne. Tonight. No more details than that."

"You think it's her? And real?" Anwyn isn't Anne. But neither do we have anyone called Anne associated with the company.

George hesitates. "It could be totally coincidental. It could be a spurious report, or common nonsense. But..."

"I can't take the chance."

Anger takes over. The arsehole Bratva mafia have been a thorn in my side for years now. The mafia boss is a nasty piece of work, barely restrained by his younger brother Artem and has been causing problems for my people that we've been constantly having to fire-fight. I accept that. Comes with the role of being the mafia everyone knows the name of in London. Westminster is the authority, making the laws and ensuring trouble is dissolved in a vat of acid. We set the example of appearing faultless, while using power to make more money than almost any other mafia in London.

The Bratva are the opposite. Uncouth, rich but brash, and with no interest in protecting those within his territory. I hated but tolerated them before.

But if they've touched my girl?

They'll wish for death when I'm done.

"Get a car ready. No need to wake anyone else, I'll deal with this."

I hang up and throw on clothes. I don't allow myself to acknowledge the fear that I might be too late. I can't be. I will be there for Anwyn. *I must.* I'll murder any and every person who gets in the way.

I'm a bad, ruthless man, but the head of the Bratva is an evil bastard. If there is even a two per cent chance they're after my girl, I'm going over there in person. And I will rip the limbs off anyone who threatens her with my bare hands.

Despite my order, my second-in-command gives me a sharp look when I arrive in the armoury. George is plucking ammunition from a box and loading it into a pistol that he shoves at me without looking.

"Sure this is a good idea boss?" he asks without inflection.

There are a staggering number of ways this is not. I take the gun, starting with the fact that if the Bratva didn't know before that I have a personal interest in Anwyn, they're about to be certain. And she's my son's ex-girlfriend. Yes.

Anwyn's student house is squeezed shoulder-to-shoulder with its neighbours in a residential street, a 1980s design that style forgot.

George grits his teeth when I tell him to stay in the car when we arrive. He doesn't like to allow me to go into a potentially dangerous situation alone, but in this case he can put up and shut up.

The front door is unlocked when I try it, and that makes me shake my head. Either I'm going to have to lecture Anwyn about security, or this is bad.

The house is quiet and dark. My feet are silent as I

creep up the stairs. No point in alerting her housemates that something is going on. If indeed it is.

Never thought I'd say this, but I really hope I'm sneaking around a girls' student house for no reason.

A door on the second floor is open, and I swear inwardly. The intel was correct.

My heart is in my throat as I look through Anwyn's door. A man dressed in black is leaning over her. I aim my gun at him, but the shot isn't clear. I'd hit my peacefully slumbering girl too.

My sleeping beauty.

There's a glint of metal and I recognise a syringe. Shit. That bastard is going to drug her. The needle is in her arm when three things happen at once.

"No." I step into the room. The Bratva kidnapper jerks up, and Anwyn's eyes fly open.

I shoot. The silencer takes most of the sound. The bastard's brains splatter over the wall behind the bed, and he collapses, dead, over Anwyn.

She lets out a sob, and sees me, her eyes wide with terror.

"Anwyn, it's okay." My voice is a gravelly whisper.

"Ben..." Her eyes roll back in her head and she slumps into the covers.

I dive forwards, and only just remember to shove the assassin's body off Anwyn but not off the bed. He's a big bastard. Can't be waking Anwyn's housemates.

The horror grips me as I gather her up in my arms. So small and delicate. She's wearing pyjamas and is as floppy as a rope, but breathing.

If I'd been another minute later. If we hadn't had that tipoff... Cold skitters over my skin at the thought. I could have lost her. If the Bratva had got her, I'd have torn down the whole of London to find her. Return her to my side, where she belongs.

Not letting her go, I frisk the pockets of the dead man, hoping for another vial. An antidote perhaps.

Nope. Blank.

It's the work of a moment to scoop up Anwyn's keys, hold her slight weight close to my chest. I work efficiently, locking doors behind us and sprinting to the car.

"Drive," I snap and arrange Anwyn on my lap as we speed away. I cradle her, my heart thudding.

She called me Ben. Probably she meant to finish that word and say Benedict. A slip of the tongue. But hell. My girl called me by my *name*.

3

ANWYN

I feel like I've been in a tumble dryer. My mouth is woolly, my head is pounding.

Prising open my eyelids, I find Mr Crosse watching me. Or is it? My vision blurs in and out.

Is this a hallucination? Or a dream?

I try to remember how I got here, or where I am. But it's dark when my eyes dart around, and I can't focus on anything.

"Anwyn," he sighs, and for once it doesn't seem to be exasperation. "Water?"

I've barely nodded before he has an arm beneath my shoulders and is helping me sit up, a glass at my lips.

His face is so close. Far nearer than we've ever been even in the last six months.

"Drink," he whispers, not taking his eyes from my face. I'm glued to him too. Or I think I am. As cool water slips down my throat, I give in to the need to stare at him.

His arm is a warm solid band behind my shoulders and he's cupping the back of my head with strong fingers.

Must be a dream. Being held by Mr Crosse? Being able

to look at him. I can finally examine his eyes the way I've always wanted to. Well, if I could keep my focus. It keeps blurring, and my eyes won't stay open. I've looked at him, covertly. But never had him look at me straight on. Not since the first night I sought refuge with him.

"Enough?" he asks gently, taking the glass away.

"So handsome," I slur out the only thought in my head.

This isn't real, because he doesn't respond to my statement. Not with horror nor even a hint of a smile. Nothing. Just keeps looking at me, his chest rising and falling quicker than usual.

I bring my hand up to his face—nope, that's his shoulder —ahhh. Yes. Slight bristles.

"Want to look ... at you." But my eyes are closing again without my volition. I have to keep them open. Really like this dream. Don't want it to end.

I want...

I'm eased back onto... a bed? It's so comfortable, and yet it's not familiar. Not the bed I use when I stay with Mr Crosse. I try to look around but my head is so heavy, my neck stiff, I can only see Benedict. His grey eyes.

"Please... Kiss..." I can't get the next word out as my vision swims.

"Sleep."

The last thing I feel before I slip back into unconsciousness is warm lips and rough stubble on my forehead.

"Fix her!"

I'm too groggy to open my eyes.

"...Have to be patient." A soothing voice.

"...Not a patient man, Doctor..." That's... That voice, it's brusque and commanding. Grumpy. Home. He's the sound of home. Then a name. It's Benedict Crosse, snarling. "Make her well, or suffer the consequences."

I try to move, and say I'm fine. He doesn't have to worry about me. I'll be out of here in a moment. It emerges as a whimper.

Footsteps approach and I prise open my eyes to see grey wool-clad legs before my vision swims and spirals.

"Anwyn."

My hand is held, strong fingers clasping mine and a thumb brushing over my knuckles.

There's a sound like a wounded animal. Then black.

This time when I wake, I merely feel like I've been beaten up. My head aches a bit, but although I wince as I open my eyes the nausea and fog have cleared.

The room is painted in charcoal grey shadows and peach sunlight. I look around cautiously.

I'm in a bedroom. It's old-world luxury. Deep green and black patterns and brocades, paintings with wide gold frames on the wall, and the scent of a forest and moving water. This one room is the size of the entire ground floor of the student house I live in.

Where am I?

The crisp white sheets rustle as I try to drag myself into a sitting position. I'm weak as a kitten.

"You're awake."

Benedict Crosse unfolds himself from a chair right beside me. The light spilling in from a gap in the curtains reveals half of his face, and my heart flips.

His expression is grave and he looks... Honestly if I

didn't know better I'd say he'd been up for two days straight. He seems exhausted. Wrecked, and a little over-intense. His grey eyes are silver, and the peachy light brings out the flecks of white in the hair at his temples and in the stubble that covers his jaw. He hasn't shaved, I'd guess for a couple of days, and Mr Crosse is always perfectly shaved. He gets a five o'clock shadow, sure, but he is invariably in a suit, controlled.

Mr Crosse is basically a businessman from a men's razor advert.

Except, right now he's not. He's the suggestive after-shave advert, all rough sex appeal and smouldering rough-ness. He's popped open his shirt collar and removed his tie. His hair is mussed too, as though he's been running his hands through it. There are dark circles under his eyes.

"What time is it?"

He checks the solid watch on his wrist. "Nine."

I nod. Well that's embarrassing. I've clearly overstayed my Sunday morning welcome. "Sorry I slept so late. I'll get up."

"In the evening, darling." The corner of his mouth kicks up. "And you're staying in bed."

"Wait it's..." There's a tickle in my memory. "What day is it? And what happened?"

"It's Monday night. And there was an attempt to kidnap you," he replies calmly.

I blink.

Someone tried to kidnap me?

I scrabble backwards up the bed, until my shoulders bump into a panel. The image of a gun in Mr Crosse's hands, pointed towards me, flickers.

"A successful attempt." My voice is wobbly, but at least my vision is clear again. Except for the minor detail of the sight of Mr Crosse at my bedside being overwhelmed by the dread that's congealing in my memory.

I'm pretty sure Mr Crosse pointed a gun at me and I've ended up with him, somewhere that isn't my house.

Sounds a lot like kidnap.

"You were in danger." He's implacable. Unmoved.

I replay the incident in my mind, as best I can. It all happened so fast. A noise that woke me. The pain in my arm. I grasp my upper arm where, yes, it is a bit sore, and find a smooth hydrocolloid dressing over the skin.

"It happened then."

Mr Crosse nods.

Another flash of recollection: the sudden weight of a man's body slumped over me, knocking my breath away. The air is fire in my throat.

"The man," I croak. "Is he dead?"

"Yes." And Mr Crosse doesn't sound at all regretful. Not even slightly.

"Was he one of your...?" I'm not certain what I'm asking.

His lip curls. "Not mine. Some... rivals who wanted to hurt me by taking you."

How would that impact Mr Crosse? "They thought taking your son's ex-girlfriend would affect you?"

He looks stricken and the sequence of last night runs on like a movie I was half watching, until I remember. *Oh no. No-no-no-no-no.*

"That's it, yes." His tone is excessively mild. He presses his lips together.

Of all the humiliating times for my massive crush on Mr Crosse to emerge from my mouth.

I told him he was handsome.

I asked him to *kiss* me.

I close my eyes. Maybe it would have been better to be kidnapped by Mr Crosse's rivals, dumped at sea with hungry sharks, or stranded in a jungle with a ravenous panther. I'm wearing *pale pink* pyjamas. Something wild and dangerous eat me now, please.

No, I mean, not like that, and yet, yes, like that. Ugh. My brain.

"Fine." I roll out of bed. From about a thousand angles this is something I'd prefer to forget.

"What are you doing?" And there's a note of genuine panic in his words.

"I'm going home." My legs aren't wobbly, just a bit out of practice, but I get to the door. I yank it open one inch before Mr Crosse reaches me and slams it shut, trapping me between his forearms, his towering body, and solid wood.

"You're not leaving," he growls.

Heat flares over my skin as he looks down at me, and I look over my shoulder at him. I want the kingpin so much. My nipples pebble, and I'm half a second from climbing him like a particularly attractive tree.

I practically drooled over him last night. And yeah, I'm doing it again. My cheeks flush.

"Let me go."

"It's dangerous."

It is here too. The warmth of his breath on my neck makes me weak. I turn in his arms, tilt my chin, and look up into his face. "Then give me a reason to stay."

His jaw clenches and a frisson of fear goes down my back. Fear of what nearly happened last night and that if I leave here there's no option but to give up everything I've built in London—my degree and my modest little job in the coffee shop. Chats with my fellow barista, Lina, and the happiness and fun and quiet companionship of being with Benedict, because he's right that another London mafia is after me. Fear that Benedict hasn't got anything more than the most tepid, cool emotion towards me when I burn every night. When I can't sleep for wanting him. Or worst of all, that maybe this isn't one-sided, but he won't confess his feelings out of loyalty to his son. That Tom is more important than I will ever be to him.

"I can't, Wyn. I can't." He leans closer, holding my gaze, a mixture of longing and torture. His arms shift until there's nothing in the world but Benedict, surrounding me. His scent is intoxicating.

"Why not?" I breathe, trying to get all of his smell into my lungs, like I could trap it there.

"You're my son's girlfriend—"

"Ex-girlfriend," I correct him.

"This is wrong."

I keep piling up mistake upon mistake. Idiot.

I'm not staying here for more humiliation, even if it is entirely my own fault this time. I duck under his arm and pull at the door as there's a click.

It doesn't budge, and it's a second before I see the glint of metal. A key.

"Give me that."

Benedict goes to pocket it, then as I reach down holds the key above his head, way higher than I can grasp but instinctively I try, too ashamed and angry to restrain myself. I grab his arm and try to pull his clenched fist to me, and he groans, stepping backwards.

Then he's across the room, shoving open a window and I'm speechless as he tosses the key out.

A small tinkle says it has reached the ground outside.

"Neither of us can leave now." For a second I swear he's

going to smile, but immediately his expression is grave again.

I dive to the window, but I already know what I'll see. This room is adjacent to the one I've slept in every Saturday for the last six months. And yeah, two floors below is the patio I've spent evenings lounging around on, reading smut and sipping mocktails.

All this time, I slept only a wall away from Benedict.

I wonder if he heard me...

My face heats. I bet he's known all along.

"Just wake someone up!" I hiss. My body is aflame with desire after touching him, and I'm going out of my mind. I cannot stay here. I'll die of horny embarrassment, which is not the way I wanted to go. I'm trapped with a man who doesn't want me, who has seen my pyjamas. "You have guards. Get them up here, tell them you've been an idiot and dropped the key out of the window, and let me out."

"No," he replies in that scary mafia kingpin voice that makes me go still. The tone he uses when he tells me to eat a piece of fruit for breakfast, or finish reading that chapter on leaf morphology before I turn in for the night. "And you're not going to scream either. Even if you did, they wouldn't do as you asked, because they work for me."

Usually, he uses that voice and I go to mush. It makes me instinctively obey. I do whatever he says because it's so dominant. A dark, rough growl that vibrates through my body.

And yeah, it does all that delicious vibration this time too, but I'm pissed.

"You can't just kidnap me and hold me prisoner," I seethe.

"Yes. I can," he replies implacably.

"No!" I grab fistfuls of his shirt and force him around to

look at me, and in my still partially dozy lack of spatial awareness, I misjudge the distance between us. The precise gap that we both maintain so carefully. Two inches or a foot, a big enough space that I don't know what it feels like to touch him.

My front presses to his. My forearms are on his sculpted chest, my breasts touching the top of his abdomen, my hips on his thighs. And nudging at my belly is a solid length.

And suddenly I know he's not so unaffected.

He's hard. The significance clubs me around the head.

Benedict Crosse wants me. Me.

I've gone six months thinking my inappropriate crush, which worsened week after week, was just that. Unrequited. He's a powerful man, and he could have anyone. He's twenty years older than me, experienced and with an air of authority that has me light-headed.

But he's got an erection, and he has trapped us together in this room for... Well at least a few hours. He looks like he sat by my bedside while I slept off whatever they drugged me with. And suddenly, I don't want to leave. I think I'm in exactly the place I should be.

I boost onto my tiptoes and lean into his warmth. Oh god his cock feels so big. I squirm a little and I'm gooey between my legs.

"We're going to be together all night, Ben." I dare to use his name. "Tell me why they were after me."

He swallows and shuts his eyes. "Because you are precious to me."

Precious. I'm dizzy with that one word.

I'm *precious.*

He killed a man who was trying to hurt me. My insecurities could find plenty of reasons to doubt this, but I don't let them. Fingers crossed for foolhardy.

I pull on his shirt, dragging him down. For a second he's immovable, an oak tree versus a hummingbird. Then with a groan, he lowers his head and takes my mouth.

And when I say takes, I mean that literally. His hand goes to the back of my neck, and his tongue plunders. I'm helpless against the force of his unleashed passion.

As if I'd protest. I try to get closer, to give as good as I get, but he doesn't give me a chance. Our mouths are sealed together, and he holds me to him, my breasts crushed and heat flaring everywhere across my skin.

He drives me backwards and I think he's going to push me to the bed, but he pivots so my back is against the door and he's holding me, braced. He strokes my cheek with his thumb, fingers in my hair and whispers my name like it's a prayer as he runs his hand up and down my side, teasing against my breast. His body traps me in place, his hard length digging into my belly and I've never felt anything so swoony in my life.

"Anwyn, we shouldn't do this," he says, then covers my lips again in a punishing kiss. He's shaking, I realise. He wants me so much he can't contain his need. That fills me with heady power. All this time I've been miserable because he didn't want me and thought I'd have to grovel for the smallest acknowledgement of his affection. His impersonal protection he gives freely, but this? Up-tight, grumpy Mr Crosse? The head of the most influential and important mafia in London does not lose control.

He does with me.

I'm held as he kisses across my face and down my neck.

"This can't be happening," he growls, but doesn't stop. The sensation of his rough stubble on my jaw makes me weak and heated between my legs.

"Ben, it is," I whisper, because I'm done with denial. I've pined after Benedict Crosse for six months.

"We mustn't." But this time, he stops, slamming his palms on the door both sides of my head. "I can't betray..."

"No one will ever know." I'm not saying my ex's name right now, and I think Ben doesn't want to either.

"Fuck..." He dips his head and closes his eyes. A pulse beats fast in his neck.

There's a long moment and for all the time I can see him fighting with himself. His sense of honour battling with his desire.

He eases back and I restrain a sob. No. No...

His eyes catch me as I'm falling into despair.

"Just tonight."

My heart does an awkward, flopping flight. A swoop of happiness and a slam down onto hard ground. A young bird trying to fly. He wants me, but only for one night.

I nod, quick. Eager.

"No one can ever know. Especially not my son."

The hurt that I'm something dirty, that he'd be ashamed of being with me, is another test flight for my fledgling heart. A secret is deliciously naughty. His. Private and cherished.

But the reference to his son? Ow. Stubbed toe and period cramps levels of ouch.

"One night, to get it out of our systems," I say, because that sounds worldly and experienced. In fact, it's just something I've read in romance books.

He sighs deeply, as though this arrangement is causing him considerable inconvenience. Well, listen up buddy. I'm inconvenienced by him being a mafia lord and kidnapping me and keeping me captive, not to mention wanting him for the past six months. We all have to deal with the challenges life throws at us.

"I'm too old and dangerous for you, Anwyn," he grinds the words out, rough and low. "Say no, as you should, and I'll tuck you back under the covers and sit by your side as you sleep."

I trail my fingers down his chest. "Give me a reason to stay awake."

He nods slowly. "Get on the bed."

4

BENEDICT

She scrambles to obey my barked command.

I don't allow myself to think about how wrong us acting on our attraction is as I look at her. All the reasons this is taboo are faded, a distant hum compared to the immediacy of *her*. Eagerly climbing onto my bed, waiting for me. And I can't deny that when I don't remember exactly why this is wrong, the lure of the forbidden makes her all the more appealing.

"So beautiful," I murmur as I sink down to sit on the bed before her. We have all night, so I gaze into her eyes and curl a blonde tendril around my finger. Incredibly soft. Her expression is trusting now, open and curious.

I sweep my hand into the silk of her hair, and gently draw her to me.

Our lips meet. A questioning, slow kiss, this one. A prelude of music, testing both players. Hot breath and supple skin. Everything about her is soft. The skin of her cheek is a contrast to my own as our mouths brush. Where I'm harsh, she's yielding.

I'm slow in deepening our kiss. First coaxing her mouth

open, then dragging my lips over to dally at her cheeks. By the time I slip my tongue in to touch hers, she's whimpering and has crept forwards. Sweet, so sweet.

Drawing her to sit over my lap I allow myself to roll my hips, my aching shaft pressing into the yielding part of her belly.

Her hands find the back of my neck and my shoulders, timidly exploring and anchoring herself as our kiss intensifies.

I've never been so turned on by a mere kiss. It's because she's Anwyn: the sexiest woman I've ever met, and the bravest. From turning up at a mafia boss' home because she needs refuge, to taking kidnap and being drugged in her stride, with no screaming or panic, Anwyn is stronger than most people twice her age.

I've had almost a whole day to absorb that my innocent girl has a tattoo of leaves over her breast, peeking out from her strappy top. I've been entranced by the revelation of her hidden self since I saw it when I laid her into my bed. So pretty, and clearly a reference to her study of plants as well as a rebellion. I love it and I'm desperate to see it all.

I can barely breathe as I lift off her tease of a camisole and reveal her glorious chest and the rest of her tattoo. I stroke my palm over the black ink first, admiring the art she chose before the beauty she was born with. The continuation of the pattern is fronds pointing down to her nipple, finely worked and elegant. I trace the design, then go where it leads: her breasts.

A small handful, they fit into my palms and she looks at me shyly, from under her lashes as I cup them and drag my thumbs over both of her nipples simultaneously. That makes her mew with need, so I give in and bring my mouth to the sensitive flesh I've revealed, tonguing and teasing her with gentle bites. My sweet girl.

She lets me unwrap my perfect little present. I leave slow kisses wherever I peel off clothes. I lick her skin; I'm a beast, tasting her and leaving my scent on every part. Next are her pyjama bottoms, baggy over her legs and riding low on her hips. I can't help but feel she's a gift for me as I pull undone the bow she's tied at her navel.

Mine.

I mouth the possessive word into her neck as I slide my hands over her smooth buttocks and drop the fabric down her thighs. I squeeze the creamy flesh and force her to me, flexing my hips the slightest amount to ease the need and ramp up the tension. She gasps at the sensation of hard into soft. My cock against her belly.

Mine.

For tonight, she is my captive and my lover. Mine to pleasure and protect.

If I ever doubted whether she held all of my heart, that doubt ended the instant I saw that man standing over her, *hurting* her. I almost regret killing him outright. I'd like to have the option of murdering him repeatedly, torturing him for laying a finger on her.

No one will ever hurt my girl again. Not even me, unless she asks for it. Damn but I wouldn't mind pulling her hair or smacking her bottom.

My cock is seeping precome, but all I want to do is touch her. I want to explore her body until I know every dip, every sensitive place, and sweet clever girl that she is, she understands that I need her naked, and lifts herself to wriggle out of her remaining clothes.

"Hold my shoulders," I tell her when she wobbles trying to get out of her shorts.

The good thing about being almost forty is that even though I'm aware we only have this single night together, I know not to rush. Twenty years ago—hell even a decade ago —I'd have tried to hurry. I'd have sought to do everything in these few special hours we have. Now I know that this time is a gift to be savoured, not an invitation to run towards some goalpost that would leave us both unsatisfied. I want her to remember this for years to come as a perfect introduction to how a man can make her feel.

How *I* make her feel.

So when she reaches for my trousers, although my cock aches, I let out a soft sound of disapproval and guide her away.

"No fair," she complains. "Don't I even get to see your chest?"

I sigh and I'm not sure if I'm irritated or amused, flattered or turned on that she'd like to see my body. I suppose it is more covered, as a rule, than hers.

"Did you mean to torture me with those little dresses you wore?" I ask as I strip off my shirt.

Her lips twitch and she fails to hide a satisfied, naughty grin as she regards the muscles I've revealed.

"Minx," I growl. "I'll make you pay for that." I drag her close again, kissing and exploring her body. She's equally greedy, still reaching between my legs.

I need to control this before it gets out of control. I trap her wrists where she has unbuckled my belt, grabbing first one hand then the other and pinning them at the small of her back. She arches into me and arousal flares from my heart to my cock at the sight and feel of her caught. Under my command.

Completely naked for me. I can't get enough of touching her, pressing my fingers in where she's soft and nipping at her where it makes her cry out. I sweep away her hair from where it covers her breasts and give it an experimental tug. She lets out a sigh and rocks her pussy into me.

Mmm. Filing that information for later.

"Are you wet, darling?"

"Maybe."

Such a brat. A complete disobedient tease, my girl. She's perfectly diligent with her studies, but with me she can be naughty.

"I bet you are," I say between kisses. I'm going to have her thighs as earmuffs, to drown out the chant that I'm a bad man for wanting her and a worse one for taking this. Finally.

And I've got an idea about how to make this even better. Hotter. A moment I can claim her, that she won't forget.

Jealous rage sparks at the thought of some fool in the future not making her come like I'm going to. I ignore it.

Releasing her hands, I lie back on the bed, smiling at her expression of alarm and curiosity.

"I want you to sit on my face."

"What?"

"I said, sit on my face." I make my tone deep and commanding.

A snort of laughter escapes her. "I can't! I'll squish you. And I haven't showered."

"I don't care," I say roughly. I reach for her, but she resists. There's a gleam of arousal in her eyes, but she shakes her head.

"I'll suffocate you."

"Let's hope." I grasp the ripe handfuls of her arse and drag her forwards. As soon as she's within range I lunge and give her a greedy lick.

She squeaks with surprise, and holds herself away.

Nope. Not accepting that. I urge her down onto my mouth, tongue fucking her as I do.

"I've been thinking about this," I admit harshly. "About how you'd taste."

"How do I taste?" she gasps out, a thread of worry and also defiance in her words.

"Fucking delicious. The best flavour I've ever known." I stroke her thigh. "Now give me your pussy properly, darling."

She slowly lowers herself fully to my mouth as I lay my head on the sheets. I don't hesitate. I eat. I feast. I cover myself in her sweet and salty taste, gorging. I hold her in place with both hands on her plump arse as she writhes and pants.

"That's it. Ride my face," I encourage her as she gains confidence. "Use me. Give me your orgasm, it's *mine.*"

She's all mine, and her wet slit is heaven. Feeling her soft folds on my tongue and giving her this pleasure—I'm certain this is her first time and I'm savagely happy to do this for her.

We're both figuring out how she likes this, so it's not instant, even though I can feel how worked up she is. She's soaking. Her honey dribbles down my chin, and it's a fucking badge of honour.

I lick and nibble. I suck. I shove into her hole, fucking her with my tongue. I listen to her every moan and feel how she moves into some motions and stills on others. And then I find it. Firm, long licks from her tight little hole all the way over her clit. She shakes. It drives her crazy.

"My good girl." Then I go at her harder with those licks that I've discovered. She moans and I don't stop. My tongue is aching. My jaw is cramped. Don't care. Nothing will ever be as perfect as she is.

Then I get my reward.

I feel it before she cries out. A tightening. A pulse.

She sobs as her orgasm overtakes her, legs going weak, falling forward onto her hands above my head. Finally she fully rests her weight on me as I gently lick her through the jolts and shudders. The way her pussy clenches makes my cock even harder.

I'm so stupidly proud. Of her. Of myself. I'm the most influential kingpin in London, and obscenely wealthy, and I want to beat my chest that I've made my girl come all over my face.

Look, no hands needed. Ha.

She slumps and I can't hold onto restraint any longer. I lift her off my face and lay her back onto my bed, a ruined girl, all mussed hair and tired limbs.

Then I'm kneeling over her. Anwyn's eyes are hazy with lust as she looks up at me, wrecked, her hair gleaming sunshine and caramel, all over the pillow, her lower lip plump and red from where she's bitten down on it as I made her come.

I need relief. I told myself I could deal with not coming, but that was a fucking lie. I'm a beast and while I can manage not to take her virginity, I am going to mark her. I free my erection and my fist is over the leaking head, stroking up and down, enjoying the moment before her eyes even go wide.

My grip is brutal and my chest is heaving. I look at her all I want, gaze skittering from her breasts to her face, down to her exposed cunt, wet and swollen from my ministrations.

"You're so gorgeous," I tell her as the pleasure coils at the base of my spine.

"No, you are." Her hands find my fine-wool-covered

thighs, not even naked skin because I was too desperate to do more than pull out my aching cock. She burrows her fingers between the fabric and my skin as though she needs to feel me as much as I did her.

Over the last six months we've both kept our eyes and hands to ourselves, and now the cumulated greed is unassailable. She clasps my leg like she'd keep me here, knelt over her, knees either side of her thighs, and looks at where the hair trails down my pecs, over my abs and to my cock.

There aren't words for this moment. Everything is both of us taking what we need. A lifetime's worth of seeing each other after far too long waiting.

"I'm going to spill all over you," I grind out. "I want to see you with my seed on your lovely skin."

I swallow back the other words. Words of my desire to shove my cock in as deep and hard as it will go, right to her womb, and spill there. To breed my good girl.

"Yes. Yes, I'm yours. I want it."

This is so dirty, so wrong. I'm going to come on her face. Her breasts. I should be ashamed to make her filthy like this. So young and innocent and I've corrupted her, and now I will mark my territory.

I'm an animal as I shove my cock into my clenched hand and imagine it's her virgin pussy.

"Ben. Please."

That does it. Pleasure so intense it's almost sharp wracks through me. But I'm not so lost I can't aim at the parts I want to see white all over. Her breasts. Belly. Chin. It drips down her neck as my muscles twitch and tense.

"Good girl," I breathe.

Through the glow, I regard Anwyn. Naked. Covered in my seed. Her pert rosy nipples are stiff, and the come slowly dribbles over the curve of her peachy breast. Her skin was perfect before, but with the reams of white? With my scent all over her? Even better.

Mine.

The best moment of my life is the pleasure combined with that sign of possession. Or perhaps that was making her come, on my mouth and so intimate. Who knows. I love seeing her like this, her eyes bright and a smile curling at the corner of her mouth, confident and sexy.

"You look so pretty painted with my seed," I say eventually. And yeah, that's the right comment as she breaks into a grin. Happy. And I return the smile, hope a bubble that encompasses us both to float into the velvet night sky.

I gather her up into my arms, her legs gripping my waist, and it's messy. Ejaculate smears onto my pecs. Her wetness brushes my lower stomach. She buries her face in my shoulder and wraps her arms around my neck as I carry her to the bathroom.

I sit on the edge of the massive claw-footed roll top bath as it fills, holding her spread on my lap, collapsed onto me. I stroke her back and the sticky wetness I spilt over her glues us together. As steam fills the air, clouding the room, I whisper that she did so well and how much I liked feeling her pulse and writhe. How I want to do it again, and make her scream louder.

The words I restrain are those of love. How I want to be all her firsts and her always, how she owns my torn and hardened heart, however worthless it is. Keeping this physical is the only way to survive it. I tangle my fingers in her blonde hair and tell her she's such a sexy good girl.

I lower her into the bathtub when it's full, and when I'm about to ease away, she grabs my hand.

"You get in too."

"Wrong way around, darling. I give the orders," I rumble.

"Please?"

The one thing that will melt me. I'm already pushing off the last of my clothes as she looks up with those big blue eyes. I'd bow to her. Only her, a queen for a kingpin.

I focus on not crushing her as I step into the bath at her back. She can't know how much I need her, because this isn't forever. Scarred, brutal men do not hold onto women like Anwyn. Sweet. Innocent. I'm undone by her, and I suspect my heart is in my eyes now the lust is temporarily slaked. Clever kitten that she is, she'll notice the change. Six months I've kept all possessive instincts under wraps, and one damn night has blown it apart.

I keep her facing away from me and wash every inch of her body. I pull her to lie on my chest and contentment seeps into me as I care for her and have her close. Her pretty breasts, made for my hands, get more than their fair share of washing until she's moaning and rubbing her arse onto my hardening cock.

When we're both rinsed, the strokes get less to do with being clean, and more for the enjoyment of pinching her nipples and stroking her clit. The flutter of her pleasure as I make her come again is stabler ground.

I can segment my love for Anwyn and my need to protect her away from the demands of my cock. I have to. That my heart wants her snuggled against me, skin to skin, is more problematic and I block that off.

I hold her as she shakes and pants and when she's bone-less, I lift her from the water and indulge in patting a towel over every curve. She's exhausted, eyelids shutting and leaning against me.

"Should I go...?" she asks as I lean over to pick her up.

"No." She belongs with me. I sweep her into my arms, bringing her back to the bed and laying her in the middle. "Stay here tonight."

"But—"

"No." Absolutely not. The uncertainty in her sleepy voice kills me. "Until we get the door unlocked in the morning, we're together. That was the deal."

One forbidden night. The only question is: how will I ever let her go?

5

ANWYN

I should have slept soundly after all the terror and drugging stuff. And I do. But it's punctuated by the feeling of Benedict's warmth and his hard frame. When I awoke, he did too, his mouth finding mine, languid and sweet, and his hands skimming down my body. I don't know how many times he fingered me to orgasm last night.

A lot.

I've had many unexpected wakings in the last forty-eight hours, but this one is the best. Ben is asleep. I get to look at him, up close. The sheet is around his waist and he's naked, sprawled on his back, one arm loosely clasping my shoulder.

I carefully lever up onto one elbow, moving slowly so as not to wake him. My kingpin is even more gorgeous than I had realised and I catalogue each part. The black stubble that covers his jawline and down to the protrusion of his Adam's apple. His eyes are closed, long lashes fanned on his cheeks. The eyebrows which are usually pinched down in a scowl are relaxed. The lines of silver at his temples glint. His chest is gloriously naked.

That happy trail... Ugh so good. Dark hair down his sculpted abdominals like that should be illegal. He's practically a honeytrap. Irresistible physically, but add in his smooth dark voice, the way he told me I'm his good girl, gives me dinner, and listens to everything I say, I've no chance. And I'd be lying if his power wasn't heady. He's the most noteworthy mafia boss in London. The man everyone looks to for permission to do anything.

And he wants me. A nothing-special girl with no family, who likes books way too much and is a bit—alright a lot—of a nerd.

My first proper kiss. My lips are tingly and plump from the force of his passion. The ones on my mouth, yes, and also the lips at my core. Benedict Crosse demanded I ride his face until I came, and I did it.

Who is this Anwyn, because I'm pretty sure she's not me.

Or, a little voice suggests, *maybe this is you, and no one else has ever seen you like he does.*

The daring voice that could get me into trouble.

I run my hand down his chest, tracing the soft and wiry hair of that happy trail.

The sheet has a lump in it. His cock. My mouth waters as my fingers brush back the fabric, so near to touching him as I've longed to do. Finally.

"Anwyn." A dangerous snarl, and Ben traps my wrist between his palm and his belly. "That's enough."

"I can make you feel good," I say, desperation beating in my heart. I can't leave him, having made me twist up with pleasure, hard and unsatisfied. He has to break apart too. "I want to lick you."

"It's morning."

I don't understand why his tone is harsh and why that's significant for a moment.

Then it rushes back.

He's my ex's *dad*. This is taboo. Wrong.

No. I don't accept that, and he doesn't want this to be over. I can tell by the gravel in his voice.

"It's still the night if we haven't got out of bed yet," I try, rubbing my thumb over his skin.

For a second our eyes meet, and I swear I see the world reflected back to me. He's trying for stern and unfeeling, but there's a tumult of pain and desire in his expression.

Then he shutters, a wall of black onyx crashing between us. "One night, Anwyn."

He puts my hand away from him and rolls off the bed, stalking across to a wardrobe where he's pulled on boxers and is buttoning a shirt before I catch up.

"That's it?" I whisper.

"Yes." He doesn't look around.

"We're going to pretend nothing happened?"

"No one can know."

I'm dried out and brittle, dead. I'm a leaf cut from a tree, wilted, scorched, then crushed beneath Benedict Crosse's well-shod heel.

Fuck him.

Really. Fuck him for making me love him even more, floating me up into the air, high on pleasure, then cutting the spell and letting me crash down to the ground.

I find my pyjamas and when that's not enough covering, I don't even ask. I barge him out of the way of his wardrobe and the first shirt that reaches my hand goes over my head.

It smells like him and my heart aches.

"Are you going to call someone to get the key and let us out?"

He doesn't answer and after a few seconds I look at him. Standing in his usual pristine suit, this one pale grey with a white shirt. He has fully dressed, tie and cufflinks included, and transformed into the immaculate, controlled mafia king of Westminster, rather than my patient lover of last night.

This is not a man who would call me his good girl and give me orgasms.

"The key," I repeat.

A muscle ticks in his jaw and he strides to the bedside cabinet and yanks it open.

"You had a spare all this time?"

"Of course," he replies calmly.

"You arsehole!"

I don't know why I'm so angry about this. He's the one who threw the key out the window after all. I was always the captive. But knowing it was there makes it all feel sordid. Like he was humouring me.

"Give it here." I snatch the key from him and my hands are shaking as I unlock the door and try to flee. I storm downstairs, and it's only as I get to the generous hallway that my brain catches up. His room is right next to mine. That's why it was so easy to find my way out of this otherwise impenetrable house.

All this time when I've spent the night here, he was just next door. A few feet and a whole world away.

I hate him.

And love him. Tears prickle behind my eyes and the room swims as I drift to a halt. The front door will be locked. I have no shoes, money, or key to get back into my house. No phone, either. I'm wearing nothing more than Ben's shirt. If I could even get out of here, I'd be stuck walking two miles home across London streets that if I'm lucky will cut my feet but not give me a deadly infection.

Yay. So potentially, I would have survived one kidnap and escaped another, only to be brought down by a lack of street cleaning and inadequate public health measures. Fun.

"I bought you a house."

I turn to find Ben right behind me, cool as you like. Fucker. He's silent as a cat. I'd put a bell on him if he were my pet.

But he's not mine, is he? And I don't know what he's on about. A house?

"Let me out." I'm resigned, trying to be as unfeeling as he is, when I'm overflowing with emotions. I'll take my chances with the walk.

"Not while the Bratva still know where you live, and have access from your housemates."

"I'm going home," I insist. "Today."

"You are ho—" He cuts himself off, shoves his hands in his pockets and takes several deep breaths, head bowed. "Tomorrow. The lawyer said your house would be ready tomorrow, and I'll deal with the Bratva..."

My expression must be as thunderous as I feel, because he sighs and adds, "Alright. Today. This evening, you get a new home. I'll get George to pick up your things—"

"I can get my own stuff," I say, instead of asking why Benedict Crosse bought me a house. I wonder what it's like? A property only for me, that I could go to whenever I want? Mad.

"No. You can't."

I remember the last time I was in my room, and shudder. Yeah. Okay, maybe he's right.

"I don't want to lose my deposit," I mutter.

He nods. "You'll get your deposit back. Or the equivalent. And if you stay here until tonight, you'll have a place of your own."

"Payment for my compliance, and not reporting you to the police?"

"If you choose that interpretation. The police do what I say. But I'm offering you safety, Anwyn, if you can just be pliant enough to take it."

It's not security I desire, it's him. I bite those words back. "Fine. I want breakfast," I grumble.

A sad smile tugs at the lips I kissed last night.

It's much like our Sunday mornings together, except I'm aware of what he looks like without clothes on.

Which, you know, is an issue. It makes me hungry, but not for the treats he sets out. Sweet and milky Darjeeling tea, toast with lashings of butter and marmalade.

Over the past six months, a wall between us had come down, chipped away, brick by brick.

We've lost all that intimacy. Every casual laugh and shared smile. We'd started telling each other truths and revealing details of our lives without even noticing. I'd told him about my studies and he'd spoken about the petty squabbles of the other mafias that he adjudicated.

It's only when we sit across from each other in silence but more physically aware than ever before that I feel how far we'd come and how much I long for its return.

I spread deep red cherry jam over a piece of toast. Ben's eyes follow my hands as I take a bite. He's staring at my mouth as I chew and his eyes go dark when I lick the jam from my lips.

It's lewd and forbidden, how I feel about him. But we said one night, so although I'm desperate to ask what his watching me means, I don't. I sip the tea he made me and consider the last thing he said.

"Tell me about the house." Because rich as this man is, buying me a home is still... Significant. To someone like me, whose main family has been a boarding school and primary home—homes—shared with dozens of others, it's the promise of spring after the longest winter. I love visiting Ben here. Powerful kingpin he might be, but his house is always calm and quiet, unlike anywhere I've lived before. Just him and me, despite the fact I know he has dozens of staff.

"It has a big garden." He frowns. "Trees and stuff."

My hand stills halfway in bringing toast to my face. A garden. A place to grow plants of my own and sit in the sunshine. My throat goes dry.

"There's a breakfast room with French doors that lead to a terrace with long stone troughs full of plants."

"Herbs?" I choke out, because in my imagination that's what a fantasy house has. Fragrant pots of lavender and rosemary and mint, and a deckchair that I lie in. An umbrella so I can see my laptop screen as I work, bare legs stretched before me.

He raises one eyebrow in an eloquent statement of *how would I know, you're the plant expert*. "I noticed the purple one that you like."

Lavender then. The rest of the house might be a wreck, but I'm already entranced.

"Is that why you bought it?" I joke.

"Yes." A simple reply, his expression serious. I don't know what to make of it, because yes, he's observant. I told Ben I liked morello cherries once, and the next Sunday morning there was this jar on the table.

Nothing escapes his notice.

But maybe this is more than his professional diligence?

"It's just outside London," he continues.

My heart jumps again. Close enough that I could visit him. I could continue to see him.

"So you can finish your studies."

Oh.

My heart snaps, a tender shoot from a seed broken off before it can reach the light. This doesn't make me special.

Probably lots of girls would be too proud to accept a gift like a house, but I'm not going to argue when someone is offering me what I've wanted since I was old enough to comprehend what a home was, and that I didn't have one. Just a place to live.

Many things have changed since the time I first dreamed about a home and a family to love. Not least, all those fuzzy dreams have sharpened into focus. Not just a home, but a townhouse in Westminster. Not just a family, but children with big grey eyes. Only one person to love me: him. Ben.

"Thank you, Mr Crosse."

There's a beat of silence.

"Back to this," he mutters. "You called me Ben last night."

"You gave me orgasms last night," I retort.

He sighs and runs his hands through his hair in a gesture of such frustration I almost feel sorry for him. Almost.

Then I remember that he thinks I'm too young and girlish to deserve more than one night of his attention.

This tension between us is horrible.

"When did you get the house?" I ask, more to fill the silence than anything else. I expect him to say it was part of some mafia deal and he had it lying around like normal people have a scattering of coins. Might have found it down the back of his sofa, Ah! That's where I lost the gold bullion and a four-bedroom house.

But he doesn't. He gulps tea and says, "Yesterday morning. I searched online for hours while you... It took me a while to find what I wanted. I'd been thinking about it for a while, not actioning it because..." His mouth twists and he trails off again, so unlike him. He's usually crisp and concise with his words. "It was imperative. I saw I'd already waited too long."

He bought me a house while I was asleep in his bed.

"Trying to get me out of here." I attempt a laugh but I'm just broken and trampled. I thought... I was so sure last night that he felt something for me.

Turns out that something was guilt.

"Trying to keep you safe, darling. From the Bratva. And from myself," he adds softly.

Safe from him? I'm not a child to be dictated to. Of all the arrogant things. And to call me by a sweet endearment, teasing me with everything he's withholding? That. That's the worst.

"Don't call me darling unless you mean it."

"I mean it." I look up and his eyes lock with mine across the table. He sets down his tea and focuses entirely on my face. "You are my one good girl. My darling. My queen. Even though we can't be together, Anwyn, you'll *always* be my darling."

The heat of my anger grows into a blaze of love and arousal, only tempered by the acknowledgement that we can't be together. "Really?"

"Yes."

And yet in the way he stands straight and folds his arms I recognise he's not going to change his mind. The honour of

Westminster and the legacy of his son mean more to him than being with me.

"I'll arrange some clothes for you, and whatever else you need. Then this evening, I'll take you to your new home."

I nod my acceptance and tentatively, we're friends again despite all that has happened in the last twenty-four hours.

It's less than an hour and a whole wardrobe's worth of clothes arrive for me. Everything I might want, all in my size. I pick out a white sun dress with buttons down the front to wear, and brush my hair so it flows over my shoulders.

As we relax into the day, me stealing books from his library and him having a series of phone conversations that amount to plans to kill the Bratva, I see how it could be. It's just as comfortable as it's been all along, but with the extra intimacy that has developed since last night.

I love him.

I can't go back to seeing him only once a week.

We have lunch, and Ben fusses—if that's the right description for dark scowls and pointed looks—over whether I've eaten enough. The day goes by far too fast, and anxiety puts out suckers in my tummy, twining and curling around me, trying to choke the air from my body.

The evening, he said. He'd take me to this beautiful house he bought me, and I won't have an excuse to visit every week.

I thought I was okay with this plan.

But the edge of the cliff is approaching fast. The moment when I'll never see Benedict Crosse again. And that is when I change my mind. I have only a few hours left with him then I'll be out of his life forever.

There's only one thing to do: what he did to me.

Last night he undid me with sheer pleasure. My body

was no longer my own. He showed me that no one will ever make me feel as good as he does, and covered me with lines of his come. He made me his in all the ways that matter, except one.

He claimed me.

Turnabout is fair play. *I'm* going to claim *him*.

6

BENEDICT

She's a rainbow of emotions. A pretty way of describing how she's been by turns furious, sad, elated, and now there's a glint in her blue eyes. Violet. An endgame and I don't know what to make of it.

This is the first time we've spent a whole day together—not counting my sitting with her when she was unconscious. I've wished for more time with her, and while this isn't what I had in mind, I'll take it.

"Is it just me, or is it hot in here?" Anwyn looks at me from under her lashes, and pulls off the cardigan, leaving only that white sundress. Hardly any more flesh exposed, really. Just her arms, and shoulders. Okay, and the valley between the swell of her breasts. The neckline reveals the tattoo. I haven't spent enough time looking at it to trace the design from memory. I should have.

She saunters over to my desk, and I'm hypnotised by the sway of her hips. The floaty dress catches between her thighs and I suppress a groan.

"What are you doing, Anwyn." I make the words harsh

and the tone worse because my cock, which was already halfway to being hard, is now a steel rod.

"I was just thinking..." There are buttons down the front of the dress and I basically have a heart attack as she trails her fingers over them and leans over my desk.

That's when I recognise this emotion from the range she's going through.

Denial.

She's not going to give up on what we gained last night.

I should tell her to stop as she undoes first one button, then the next.

"It's hot in here."

It's not particularly, but I nod.

"I'm a bit sore..."

Alright, she's right, it is roasting. I'm light-headed. She's been through a lot in the last few days, but I'm the one that feels overwhelmed as she bares the valley between her breasts. So beautiful, I can't drag my eyes away.

"Would you check something for me?" She has never smiled at me like this before, slow, wicked, and seductive. Sliding around the table, she perches on the edge, bare legs over mine. Arousal is flowing through me and into my dick. I swear it must be leaking precome. There's a flyaway whisp of honey-blonde hair on her cheek and yeah, I want to brush it tenderly away. I also need to greedily scoop up all those silky strands and hold her as I fuck her so thoroughly she cries.

"Here." She drags the hem of her dress up.

It should be my hand doing that. Undressing her. I clench my fists. To think I used to say Anwyn's mere presence was torture.

What a naive man I was.

This. *This* is true suffering. To know what her cunt

tastes like, and not be able to lose myself in her sweetness again, because if I did I'd be a shitty father and a bad example to the whole of my territory. She's half my age.

She shifts so the top of her thigh, then the seam of her knickers is revealed and I can't breathe. It's all I can do to stop myself from reaching and pulling her onto my lap. I drag my gaze up to her face and there's challenge there. Glittering defiance.

"Have I got bruises?"

"No." I keep my gaze trained on her blue eyes. I'm going to drown in her and I don't even care.

"You have to look," she replies teasingly. "What about here?" A brush of fabric on skin, and without my volition I'm staring at her pert arse cheek where it's exposed by her pulling up her little lacy knickers.

The knickers I bought for her.

I wonder if my cock will ever be soft again. Perhaps I'll explode? The ache is practically a burn now. It's taken over my whole body. I'm throbbing.

"Well?" she prompts me. My naughty minx. I catch her glancing at where she's made me very obviously hard, and shit. This is playing with fire.

"No." I drag in a breath like I've been trapped underwater. "You're not bruised." Thank god. I managed not to bruise her last night.

I will not feel disappointed that I didn't leave a mark on her. I will not.

"Appreciate you checking." She toys with the hem of her dress, letting it slide down.

Okay, that's a bit more air in the room, but definitely disappointing. The sweet curve of the bottom of her arse, damn I'd look at her all day.

"I'd like to repay your kindness."

"No thanks needed," I grind out. "And I'm not *kind*." I'm a slathering horrible monster.

"Maybe you need someone to be kind to you then. As an example." She brushes her hand over the obvious bulge in my lap.

"Anwyn," I say, the warning loud.

"I want to taste you, Ben."

Ah fuck. She undoes me when she says my name.

"Let me make you feel good." She leans over me. "Like you did for me last night."

Words roll around in my head. I don't speak.

"I could use my mouth. I didn't have the chance to do that." A hint of uncertainty, a pinch of yearning. The idea of my girl missing out on anything she wants is unthinkable. She can have everything.

"Go on then." I barely recognise my voice. There's authority, yes, but the rasp is all desire. "Get to your knees."

She slides down eagerly, eyes shining with anticipation.

"Take out my cock."

I think I intend to scare her, but as her lips part I slide my hand into her hair so very gently. As soft and tender as she deserves, even as I struggle not to shake. Her small hands on my belt. The tightening at my waist, then my trousers settle, looser. The button pops. The sound of the zip is a purr. She takes every movement with tentative slowness. Unfamiliar with a man's clothing.

She's so arousing, it's unreal. The combination of eagerness and innocence.

She shifts and I see the carpet digging into my girl's knees, and *oh absolutely not.*

"Stay there," I bark and I ignore her hurt mewl as I stride off. Cushions. For a second my brain is so fried I can't remember where in my own house I'd find a goddamn pillow, but I manage and haul two back like a caveman bringing home a kill. I toss them onto the floor.

She looks between me and the cushions and gulps. I don't know what her over-active imagination has dreamed up, but I point. "Kneel there."

Her shoulders relax as she crawls over and damn, I didn't think I could get any harder, but apparently the sight of Anwyn crawling over to kneel and be more comfortable as she sucks my cock has the capacity to make precome leak from my cock. I'm desperate.

So you'd think it would be rough as I stand before her. But while I'm tempted to shove away my clothes, pull her mouth onto my cock and thrust, I'd prefer to savour her expression when she discovers me.

Savage pride at her bravery fills me as she draws down my boxers and her thumb brushes the head. Her eyes go wide as she reveals my length.

I'm beyond being objective right now, but her hands seem little next to my erection. I'm harder than I can ever remember, which is quite something given how I've thought of her for the last six months.

"Do you like your man's cock, darling?" And though her expression was eloquent, a knot constricts in my chest as I wait for her answer.

The smile spreads across her face, lighting her eyes. She leans forwards, gaze fixed on mine and licks the tip. Once.

I jerk. That brief contact of her tongue forces a hiss from me.

"You tease," I grind out, but there's so much affection in it that she grins.

"Do you want me to suck your cock, Mr Crosse?"

My fist closes and she smirks as the action tightens her hair onto her scalp.

"Brat," I murmur as I draw her inexorably to where I need her. She gasps as I tug. "I'll get you back for this."

I will. I'm going to lick her until she screams for mercy after her seventh orgasm in a row.

Right after... Oh god.

She takes the sensitive tip of my cock between her lips and my chest compresses. My breath is stolen. The pleasure is unlike anything I've experienced in my forty years of life. Her mouth is hot and wet and soft. Her lips press over the helmet and I'm cross-eyed. I'm big. Intimidatingly so, but she's so freaking brave, and though it's obviously stuffing her mouth and she must be forcing her jaw open, she covers her teeth and it's all smooth heat.

"Deeper," I tell her, and she obeys, taking me down until my cock hits the back of her throat. Then without being told, she bobs her head and hollows out her cheeks.

"Good girl."

She whimpers and I feel her nod. Oh, she likes that, does she?

"My good girl, I love the way you're sucking my cock." I don't know who is more turned on by my words, her or me. I see a shudder go through her and reach down to find her nipple. "You like this too, don't you? Is your pretty slit wet for me?"

"Uh," she makes a noise that could be a yes or just a wordless indication of need.

"You know what good girls who have pleased their man with the way they suck his cock get?" I don't wait for her answer. "They get to receive more. I'm going to take your virginity, darling. I'm going to stretch you out, open you up, and ruin you for any other man."

I didn't intend to be so possessive, but I can't help it. She has her mouth over my cock and I want her. I want more, damn it. And wrong or not—who am I kidding, it is deliciously taboo to be shoving into a woman twenty years younger than me—I'm not stopping. She's my son's age. Even though virgins have never been my thing, with Anwyn it makes this insanely hot.

"Good girls get fucked in their mouths." I can't believe I'm saying this, or going to do it.

She moans her assent.

Ah, right. That's why. Because she's brave and strong and can take all of me. The light and the dark.

"And if it's too much, good girls tap here." I place her little hand on my thigh, even as she continues to drive me out of my mind with her tongue exploring the taut skin of my cock. "Do you understand?"

Another whimper, and our eyes meet over my glistening shaft. I card both hands into her hair, the silk holding me, as I shift so I can see as I pull her further, deeper with each thrust of my hips upwards and pull of her down. It feels like Anwyn is smooth everywhere I touch. I bet her pussy is heaven. My brain stutters on that, the taboo wrestling with how perfect this is.

She's mine. I'm the only one who will ever fuck her mouth. I'm not going to let her go. She'll never have bad sex, or heartbreak, or be messed around.

Nope. She'll be loved and cherished and given orgasms and complimented. And used too, because my dirty girl likes this.

As I fuck into her mouth, I'm unable to look away, and she doesn't let go of my thigh, digging her nails into my quads and encouraging me to take her rougher and harder than I would otherwise. Her eyes water, but her hand never wavers. Never taps. And she doesn't take her eyes off mine.

It's passionate in a way I should have known it would be

with Anwyn. The back of her throat makes the top of my cock tingle. I'm not fully in, just the head, really, but it's enough. It's more than enough with her blue eyes on me. My balls pull up, readying. Pleasure spirals low in my belly.

It's a damn good thing I feel her slight nod and her grip my leg, but that's not where I'm ending this.

"You do that so well, darling," I rasp.

A small choke from her, and I lift Anwyn's head away, a line of spit connecting us until she swallows and then licks her lips.

"Why have you stopped?" There's a hint of confusion in her open-mouthed look. Her exposed breasts heave and yes, she looks wrecked, lips red from taking my cock.

"I'm a bit old-fashioned," I say with a lopsided grin. "I'm going to mark you as mine. But tell me, darling, where would you like my seed?"

Her eyes go wide.

"Where would you prefer my seed to go, my good girl?" I rasp. "In your mouth? Over those creamy thighs you teased me with? Painting your little tits? Or going bare and deep into your pussy, and breeding you."

"Yes."

And we understand each other, this girl and I, because I don't have to clarify. She means she wants all of those.

"We will. But tell me what you want now."

7

ANWYN

In six months of spending Saturday evenings together in his office, the recurring fantasy I've had is so cliché I'm almost embarrassed.

But there's a risk this is the one and only time, so there's no room for my shyness. "Will you take me on your desk?"

He slants one eyebrow. "You want me to lay you across the table and devour you, like I've lost control?"

I nod rapidly. Oh *yeah*. That. So much that.

With a reckless throw of his arm, he sweeps everything off the shiny wood. The glass paperweight, all his reports and chunky pens, books, and even his computer peripheries of keyboard and mouse, all crash to the floor. The paperweight rolls then smacks against a bookcase, bouncing off into a rustle of papers then coming to a standstill. The quiet is punctuated by my gasps for air and Ben's deep rasps. The dark shiny wood is exposed, ready for me to be defiled.

It's what I wanted. Ben to lose control, yet I'm as horrified as I am excited. He's seen inside my head and—

"Turn around."

The shock makes me stone. But not normal stone.

Magma, heavy and burning hot. Impossible. Elemental. As with all those evenings together, he's so dominant and bossy that my clit jumps at his order.

Ben levels me with a haughty look and as my cheeks flush, I obey.

There's a pause. I know what's coming, but I wait.

"Bend over." His voice is soft and calm, but commanding.

I do that too, laying my cheek on the cool wood. And even though I'm clothed, and so is he, it feels filthy. My breasts press into the polished table, and my slit is flooded with yet more arousal at how my bottom is in the air.

"Pull up your skirt."

I quickly yank it up to around my waist, eager. I want him and everything I've dreamed of is so close, I can barely think.

"Take down your knickers." He sounds a bit hoarse, and as I slide my white lace knickers down my thighs he groans. "You're so wet, darling."

"You made me wet, Mr Crosse."

"Ben," he corrects and there's the rustle of cloth.

"Ben," I sigh. "Ben." I love both names. My sweet and caring lover, Ben. And severe, dangerous, scary mafia kingpin, Mr Crosse.

Something hard and blunt and hot touches my soaking pussy. His crown.

"Do you want me to fuck you, darling?" He strokes the blunt tip over my folds, not quite where I need him. Only brushing my entrance and skimming over my clit.

"Yes." It comes out as a whine. A cry of desperate need and I push back onto him.

He eases away with a chuckle. "Patience, my slutty girl. You want my cock, huh?"

"Yes. Please. Mr Crosse, please." Vaguely my brain registers he's bare. That he's going to fuck me raw, no condom. And hell, but that's makes my clit twitch and I writhe, mindlessly trying to get more contact to my pussy. I trust him. I want nothing between us.

"Open your legs."

I scramble to obey. I've been so busy rubbing my thighs together in an attempt to ease the ache in my clit, I kind of forgot. I shift my feet apart and as a reward he pushes further, stepping between my feet. The smooth fabric of his trousers on my bare inner thighs emphasises how naughty this is. He's fully clothed, I'm not. I'm his slut, bending over the desk to be railed by the older, forbidden man.

Getting railed in a sundress.

A powerful mafia boss who could have anyone he wanted, and has chosen *me*.

"Oh you're so pretty like this, Anwyn. Pink and lush." He almost purrs as he teases us both, dragging his cock where I'm slick. He must have his cock in his fist, and the thought makes my insides clench. Empty, so empty.

He pauses. "There's one more thing."

"Anything." I'm so focussed on the place between my thighs where he's notched into me, just the very tip resting in my folds, that I can't think.

He gathers my torso up into his arms, his hands on my belly and sternum. The coarse bristles of his cheek rub mine, and he presses a kiss next to my mouth.

"I love you," he whispers. "Once I've been inside you, I won't let you go, Anwyn. Any price, I'll pay it. The censure of the world, the anger of my son, the disapproval of your friends and my business associates. I don't care, so long as I have you as my wife."

This is what I wanted to hear, all these years. I wanted

to be enough for someone, to be loved. Benedict Crosse is willing to burn everything to the ground to have me.

"In my bed, in my life, filling you up constantly. You better ready yourself. I'm going to be insatiable unless you stop me *right now*. This moment." He stills, giving me the space to think.

Ha. No need. Threatening me with a good time, with being *his*, isn't going to put me off.

"Don't stop." I melt, arching back into him. "Please."

"You must be very sure, darling. There won't be any one-night stands or being a promiscuous student for you," he growls. "You'll be married to a beast. I'm jealous. You won't be able to touch other men, because any part of them that contacts you will be cut off."

I'm clearly as deranged as he is, because arousal shoots to my core. He wants me. I'm his possession and he isn't going to compromise.

"I want this." It's not even a question. He's the only person I want to touch me, and I want to rub against him like I'm a cat and he's catnip. He's a pretty, slightly grey drug that I can't believe I am the first one to claim. He's been on this earth forty years, being so absolutely perfect, and I'm the one he wants.

I went for a wildlife walk in the local park and found a lion that demands to be my housecat.

"Good. Then let me in, darling." Eases me forward onto the desk again, and pushes into me.

I gasp, because although I'm dripping with arousal and so turned on I'm practically glowing, there's a pinch. I'm too tight for him to enter, and for a second I panic.

Maybe this is impossible.

"I know, I know it hurts," he murmurs soothingly. "But it will feel good, I promise." He shoves my dress further up and strokes circular motions onto my back, even as he presses deeper, the constriction blooming into a delicious stretch.

"Ben, I..." I'm going to say I can't do this, but he reaches around and unerringly finds my clit. Something adjusts, slotting into place as he rubs me. The pleasure spirals up to where my nipples are hard on the table, and down to my pussy. And I'm no longer fighting him. I'm welcoming him. I need more.

"Yes, that's my good girl, Wyn," he growls over my neck, making a shiver go up and down my spine. "Open for me more. You should see how you look taking me into your slit. Beautiful."

And that's when it begins to be everything. I'm rocking back onto him, and he's groaning. He's big, and I'm tight, but I hadn't anticipated how hot and smooth he'd be. Not like a cold and impersonal toy that I've used before. When I feel his hips on my butt I know he's as deep as he can go.

I'm wrong.

The next thrust, he's deeper again. I swear I can feel him under my ribs.

I whimper something that might be his name, or a plea for more, or words of love. It would definitely be that last one if my brain hadn't regressed evolutionarily. I'm no more competent than a sensitive plant. A Venus flytrap, triggering at his lightest touch.

I grasp and scrabble at the smooth table, not even knowing what I'm lacking, but I'm a wildflower buffeted by the wind.

His hand comes down firmly on my wrist, pinning it in place. Then the other. He's caught me before I realise what's happened, and is holding both my hands onto the wood with one of his. It's like all the energy I was expending thrashing around is redirected by him, streaming it into my pussy, where I throb all over. He is pinning me, my arms in the air, his other hand stroking my clit, and his cock fills me. I'm surrounded by his touch, unable to escape.

"You're so fucking beautiful." He pulls almost all the way out, then slams back in. Again, faster, and I can't breathe for the pleasure building. It's tingling across my whole body. My breasts are squashed into the table, and so are the front of my thighs, and being trapped makes this all the hotter.

I'm his to use. His to fill and claim and breed. He's hammering into me, and there's no space for anything but Benedict Crosse in my body or my life.

"Come over my cock, Wyn." He pushes my clit more vigorously, or something, I don't even know. It just feels amazing. Overwhelming. "I want to feel you cream all down yourself. I'm going to spoil my good girl."

I can't hold out, even if I wanted to. The harder he pounds into me, the higher I spiral, until I get to the top, and burst.

My pussy pulses, hard. I think I yell.

"That's it," he croons. "You're doing perfectly. You are the best thing I've ever heard, coming and screaming like a banshee. You feel so good, coming around my cock, darling." And it sounds as though he's coaching me through a trial, but it's pleasure so intense it might split me apart.

As my body eases, I'm aware again. Not just of his impossibly large and solid cock thrusting into me, only the tip at my entrance, slowly now, almost lazily. His hands digging into my hips, the smooth wood of his desk under me.

"Oh my god." My brain is limp as a dramatic houseplant that hasn't been watered for a week. My body is a sack of feelings, all good, all his.

"My best girl." Ben leans over me, reaching out, and I stretch around to look into his face.

"That was..." There are no words.

"I'm glad." He smiles, feral and dangerous, then his eyes narrow. "But this is wrong."

8

BENEDICT

"Wrong? No," she protests.

"Shhh, shh, that's enough." I pull out of her abruptly.

A sob escapes my girl and she grasps for me even as I pull her up and turn her into my arms. Face to face, as we should be for the first time I come inside her. Breed her.

No misunderstandings because she can't see how sincere I am about this. About her.

"Mr Crosse, Ben. Don't stop. It's right," she babbles. "I swear it's right." Her eyes are wide and I think she might be about to cry.

"Silly girl," I mutter just before my mouth hits hers again. Then we're kissing, tongues tangling, and her hands grasp the back of my head, holding me to her. "Thinking I'd leave this hot wet cunt of yours before I've filled you up." I hitch her up my body—she's so petite—and sit her on my desk. Then I drive back into her hot, waiting slit.

She really shouts this time as I enter her, and I roar.

"If you and I are wrong, I never want to be right." I growl the words into her mouth around our kiss. "I don't care. I'd defy every law in every part of the world to have you. Any price, I'll pay it. Anything."

"Yes. Yes."

"You were made for me," I say as I drag my tongue over her cheek.

"I thought—"

I laugh harshly. "You thought I'd give you up? *Never*. You're mine now, Wyn. I'm going to move you and fuck you exactly as I choose."

She lets out a squeak I'm taking as agreement, since it's accompanied by a nod of her head that I feel against my ear.

"But the first time I come inside you I want you to see me, darling. Look into my eyes and see how I'm claiming this virgin cunt as mine. I'm going to watch you come again, and see your expression when I tell you I will breed you."

Her look is full of wonder. "You want—"

"I'm raw inside you. That wasn't an accident." I grab under one of her knees and bring it up until her heel is on the edge of the desk. It opens her out, as I intended. Her head falls back and she moans. I drink it in, kissing her exposed neck, biting gently as I keep pistoning into her.

"I'm going to fill you up with my come. I'm going to press the head of my cock right up to your womb and plant my seed there." I cram my hand between our bodies and indicate the place, low on her abdomen, where she'll increase when she's pregnant.

"Yes." She's shaking a bit and I love that.

"You want me to put a baby in you? You want me to make you round and ripe?" My chest constricts as I speak. I'm laying out all my dreams for her, revealing my secret wishes in dirty talk.

"Breed me, that's what you—" I cut her off, my lips silencing her.

Thank fuck.

I don't think I could stop if she'd said no. She's in my blood, this girl. I kiss her mouth as I thrust into her, relishing how soft and tight she is. The scent of her, the velvet feel. She's perfect in every way.

"Ben." She tilts her hips and I go deeper. "More."

"Six months," I grumble. "You kept this from me for six months. From *the* pussy I own. And now you're making demands."

We're so close I feel her smirk as much as see it as she digs her heels into my buttocks. We both know that I'm rewriting history in the most ludicrous manner. But right now all I can think is that she's mine, and *I could have lost her*.

If I'd got out of my own idiot way, I could have claimed her months ago and she'd never have woken to fear and death.

"Sorry, kingpin. I should have got myself kidnapped sooner." She rakes her nails across my back rough enough to make me hiss. "Punish me for it."

"I will." Gathering her hair up, I pull to reveal her tender creamy throat. I bite her. Then I slam in hard. She cries out.

I don't ask if she's okay. She is, and this is a punishment. It's supposed to have a sweet edge of pain. Again and again I thrust, using her pussy to spiral myself towards release. I'm marking her in the most primal way, sucking love bites onto her jawline and I grip the soft curve of her hip brutal enough that my fingers will leave bruises. I don't care. *No.* I'm gleeful that she'll see these marks, and her cunt will be sore and used, and she'll know she belongs to me.

The pleasure is making me crazy. I'm so obsessed with her. This is far too fast and hard for her first time, but watching every expression on her face gives me permission to use her hot wet slit to make myself feel good.

So I do. I take her forcibly, pushing the sensitive tip of my cock right into her, shoving up against the top of her passage, over and over.

"You're being such a good girl for me," I say, looking into her eyes, drowning in that blue as she whimpers in response. "You like being taken like this, don't you, my pretty girl?"

"You feel..." She trails off into a moan.

"What?" I demand.

"Huge inside me. You've..." Her breath comes out in pants.

"Go on." I'm swelling inside her further.

"Found a whole new part of my body..." Tossing her head, she's struggling to keep the thought straight. I thrust harder, an incentive to continue and a punishment for not focusing on what I've asked her. I can feel her begin to tense and it's ecstasy like I've never felt.

"I love..." The rest of her declaration is lost in a cry of pleasure as she grasps the back of my head, and holds me to her, her pussy clamps down on my cock in waves. She's coming on my cock. My girl, made speechless by how we are together.

My brain short circuits. Orgasm steals up on me without warning, pulled from me by the words she almost said and the sensation of her milking the come from me.

"I'm going to fill you up," I choke out.

"Yes, Ben." The phrase is muffled by us both wanting to kiss.

One thrust more, and I lodge myself as deep as I can and it spurts out of me in wave after wave that wrack my body. She gasps as we grip each other, me holding her arse and her keeping my forehead pressed to hers. I'm cross-eyed, but I can see her blue eyes as I spill right against her womb.

"Take it all, darling."

She lets out a squeak of agreement and digs in her nails enough to hurt. Another wave hits me at the feel of her claiming me, and I'm spent. Drained. As my orgasm ebbs away, I lift her and fall back onto my office chair, still lodged in her.

I need skin-to-skin contact. I don't know if I'll ever allow her to leave my side again. She relaxes on top of me with a contented sigh, nestled on my lap.

"You stretched me open to the light. You inside me was like sunshine after a lifetime of shade. I didn't know sex would feel like my body was finally alive."

Holding her even closer to me, I try to swallow the tightness in my throat. Because although she's the virgin here, or was, it's her who is expressing how this feels. I'm living now I'm with Anwyn.

"I love you." I never want her to doubt, so I repeat the vulnerable-making declaration. "I love you so fucking much. You're my everything, Anwyn."

"I never thought I'd have you," she confesses into my shoulder. "I thought I'd tragically carry around this unrequited love for my ex-boyfriend's dad forever. Permanent sad cat."

Even as I wince at the reminder of Tom, I choke with laughter. But I meant it. Having Anwyn is worth any price I have to pay.

"Mr Crosse!" There's a loud knock at the door, and my second-in-command's panicked voice reverberates through the wood. "Sorry to let myself into the house, but I had to get hold of you."

I frown as I spot my phone on the floor, swept away when I cleared the desk to place my girl in the centre of my life.

"What is it?" I shout.

There's a pause.

"Your son has been kidnapped."

9

ANWYN

Ben listens, pale faced, as George explains what has happened, to the best of his knowledge. The details are scant. Tom was spending a couple of days camping with a friend, and it was only when he didn't arrive back as scheduled that George realised something was up.

Then the message from the Bratva arrived. Moments later, a tip-off the same as the one that had alerted Ben to my being at risk.

"*Bring the girl* were definitely his exact words?" Ben asks again.

George nods soberly.

"It's a trap." Ben paces around the office like a caged panther.

"Obviously," George concurs.

"In what way?" I'm standing awkwardly to the side, next to the desk where Ben took my virginity not that long ago. We both threw on clothes in record time.

Nothing like realising someone might die to kill the warm afterglow. Pun not intended. Mostly.

"He knows you're my priority. But he's got my son. Get you both together, he has you both at risk, and me off-balance." Ben scowls at the floor as though if he's scary enough he'll terrify physical structures to rise up and do his bidding.

"It's going to be okay." I catch his hand as he passes me.

"For you, yes." He stops and strokes his knuckles over my cheek. "You won't be in danger."

"I'm not being left here." Whatever is happening, I'll be at Ben's side.

"You're staying here." His voice is steel.

"One, last time I was home without you I was kidnapped. Two, telling me to stay put doesn't turn out how you think it will. And three, I've got skin in this game. If my future husband and my ex-boyfriend are doing something important, you better believe I'm going to be there."

Ben grabs my hand and jerks me abruptly into his arms. A sense of calm envelops me as he presses his forearm into my back and a kiss to the top of my head. I breathe in his scent. Spicy and masculine, as well as musky. He smells like dark sex and warm pine forest breezes.

"Putting you in danger isn't worth it," Ben mutters. "I should just leave Tom to it."

"No way." And though I'm speaking into his chest and my selfish heart is gleeful that Ben would give up everything, even his son, for me, I can't let him do that. "I'm in Westminster now."

"Really?" He sounds a bit shocked. "You'd accept being part of Westminster?"

"Yes," I insist.

"This will end in bloodshed. Are you prepared for that?" He's checking, I think. Probing to see if this is something he has to give up for me.

"I know. I'm ready." That's a total lie, I'm one for plants and books, not guns and knives. But I'm going to be Benedict Crosse's wife, and Westminster is part of *him*. The kingpin and the sweet paternal figure, I love both sides. Whatever happens with Tom, I'm not having my man give up on his life's work.

He stares at me, incredulous. Minutes, days, aeons tick past. It's probably only ten seconds. A slow, pleased smile spreads across his face, lighting his eyes to silver. "I think it's time for a regime change in the Bratva." He nods thoughtfully. "I don't usually get involved with such things, but I'll make an exception. Do you want to help?"

"Yes." Fear pulses through me but I'm here. I'll be by Mr Crosse's side and in Ben's arms until the end of the world.

"Good." Just that word from him sends pleasure skittering down my spine. He pulls his phone from his pocket and opens a message. "Remind me the name of your friend at the cafe you work at?"

"Uh." I don't have any friends there. Unless you count the girl who does the shift before me. Sometimes I chat with her. "Lina?"

"Yes. Thank you." He holds up his phone and speaks into it. A voice message maybe? Or speech to text? "Artem, I'm thinking of offering Lina a job. If you don't want that, you should call me."

I frown, and Ben reaches over, smoothing my brow with his thumb. "Nothing's going to happen to your friend, don't worry. But it was recently impressed on me how significant a little pressure on a girl can affect a man."

Me. He means me. I open my mouth to ask him what happened, but he beats me to it.

"You're a clever girl. Much cleverer than the Bratva

think, Anwyn. Are you willing to work very hard for me, darling?"

"Always." I'd do anything for Benedict Crosse.

"Then I have an idea of how you can come with me. As Queen of Westminster."

We arrive at the warehouse designated as a neutral place to meet just as the colours fade into grey night. Ben has been drilling me all day. I started off not having ever touched a gun, but now I know every part by name, how to keep my arms braced, and I've taken it from the holster on my thigh a hundred times or more.

Exactly as Ben predicted, they're all patted down by the Bratva goon, and one of the Westminster men does the same to the Bratva men. Everyone is unarmed.

But when the Bratva goon approaches me, Ben growls, dark and feral.

"Touch my fiancée and it will be the last thing you do."

So low and possessive, his rumbling words send a bolt of pure longing from my throat to my pussy.

Gulping, the goon backs off.

And the gun remains in its holster on my leg. An insurance policy, Ben said. There is a plan A, and although he explained it to me, I'm... Sceptical. I guess having no family myself, I can't imagine betraying them.

The Bratva delegation is five men. The aforesaid goon and a man about my age stand together. My ex-boyfriend Tom, eyes wide and mouth taped, a man behind him. He's as tall as Ben, with black hair and I think they're about the same age. Attractive if you like jawlines so square you can cut yourself on them.

Then the Bratva kingpin stands alone. A little shorter than the other man, he has all the same features but they're mixed up differently. Two plants with lush green leaves and red berries—one poisonous, one sweet.

"What do you want, Victor?" Benedict asks from next to me.

"Your territory for your boy." Victor flicks his fingers at Tom, who is shoved to his knees by the taller man. He catches Ben's eye above my head, and there's a tense moment. The younger Bratva man is looking at the floor, seemingly impotently angry, eyes hard.

"That's unreasonable and you know it, Victor." Ben is completely unflustered. Calm. You wouldn't know he paced this afternoon, or patiently showed me time after time after time how to pull the safety off the gun I'm wearing, even as I got it wrong repeatedly.

"You want me to compromise?" Victor has a strong Russian accent, whereas his brother's is less noticeable. "I compromise. Half of Westminster for half of the boy."

He barks out a cynical laugh that makes it clear he'd enjoy cutting someone in half.

"I keep the half with The Busy Bean coffee shop. My fiancée works there, you know. I've been keeping a close eye on it. Sweet place. But you wouldn't have any access to it. No crossing the lines at all. For anyone." Ben's gaze flits between the other two Bratva family members.

"Don't," the second man says, eyes flashing.

"Shut up, Artem. If I want your opinion I'll ask for it."

Oh, that's Artem. Ben said he was Victor's brother.

"Enough talk of coffee shops," Victor snaps and points the barrel of his gun to the back of Tom's head. Tom is trembling and his grey eyes are brimming with fear as he looks to his father for comfort. To Benedict.

My stomach plummets as I realise my ex-boyfriend might die because Ben prioritised me instead of him.

This isn't going as I expected from the plan. Why has he allowed it to happen? Surely Tom is in danger?

I attempt to assess the situation, even though I have literally zero experience with this. I could pull out my gun and try to kill Victor, as Ben showed me. But if I miss, Tom will definitely die. If I hit Victor, will he be able to shoot Tom before he goes down? I have no idea. This is not my area of expertise. I am significantly better with plants.

If only the mafia all sat down and resolved their differences with who was faster at genetic sequencing, I would be a perfect asset to Ben. As it is, I'm a liability.

"Dad." The youngest of the Bratva men steps forwards. "Don't do this. Please."

I see Tom's eyes flick up to the young man with pain and hope and betrayal and I still.

He's gay, and I can read Ben's face so easily. It's Tom's choice of partner that surprises him, not their gender. Tom has been in a relationship with the Bratva.

"Shut up, Sergey." The Bratva boss doesn't take his gaze from Tom. "Crosse. It's a simple choice. What do you value? Your territory, or your son?"

"It's not that simple though, is it? I don't like the way you run your operation, Victor. You're asking me to put the lives of numerous women and children under my care over that of my own son." Ben is calm, impassive even, but I can see the war raging inside him, even as Tom's shoulders shake.

Tom makes a muffled attempt to speak, and Artem sighs dramatically, stomps over to Tom and brutally rips off the tape from his mouth with a sound that makes me wince.

Victor's hand doesn't waver as Artem steps back.

"I love you," Tom blurts out. "Dad."

"I love you, too." Ben's jaw clenches. It's taking everything in him not to cave.

"And Sergey," Tom adds quietly. "I loved you as well."

He's already talking about himself in the past tense, resigned to his death.

"Tom..." Sergey breathes, stepping forwards again, his face stricken with grief.

"You stupid p—" Victor begins, turning to his son.

"Dad, don't give—" Tom looks up.

A gunshot blasts out, and Victor slumps to the ground. Blood trickles from a hole in his temple.

On the other side of the room, Victor's goon steps towards Ben, a knife glinting, while he is focused on Artem.

The rage is instant, red hot, and furious. After everything that has happened, no one is going to take Benedict Crosse from me. I snatch up my dress, yank out the gun and fire at the man's chest, squeezing the trigger the moment I line up the sight on him. The biggest target.

The noise doesn't even register. All I can think is, *Ben*.

The man staggers, arms falling. Then Sergey races to the goon, snatching the knife from him and I'm not as quick this time, staring at my hand. That hand shot a man. Sergey doesn't hesitate. Knife in hand, he falls to his knees at Tom's side, just as Ben stops George and me, a hand out in both directions.

Sergey cuts the ties at Tom's wrists, and Tom collapses forwards, Sergey catching him in his arms. Tom's mouth finds his lover's, kissing him in a way that he never did with me, before burying his face in his neck.

There's a silence as we all watch Sergey comforting Tom.

"Thank you," Ben says softly, his eyes meeting mine,

and I'm covered in warmth. "And you too." He nods to Artem.

The gun slips from my hands. I just shot a man. I look at the goon bleeding on the floor. His eyes are open but glassy. Lifeless. My gaze springs back to Ben. I should feel bad, but there is no room for regret. I'd a thousand times rather he was dead and Ben safe.

"Well, I think that's the end of that," Artem says, pocketing a gun.

I get it now. That was what Ben meant when he said I wouldn't be the only armed person present. George deliberately didn't take one of Artem's guns when he frisked him. Ben threatened Lina in the mildest terms, and Artem murdered his brother rather than have her in the Westminster territory but forbidden to him. By Ben's account, Victor had it coming but still. Artem made a bleak choice.

"I'll be taking over the Mayfair Bratva. I hope we can deal politely with each other, Mr Crosse. I can't pretend I'm delighted that my nephew is banging your son."

Ben rolls his eyes. "That was very nearly Shakespearean. I suggest we do something to prevent such occurrences again. A London Mafia Syndicate, perhaps. I'll have invitations sent."

Artem looks down at his dead brother with distaste. "So long as they can be together without compromising the security of either of our activities, I have no objection."

"About those operations." Ben has taken this with the sort of sang-froid that makes him a terrifying mafia boss and me his student girlfriend. "I don't like—"

"Neither do I." The new boss of the Bratva nods. "You'll find I run things differently to my brother."

"Do you want to take that corpse, or shall I have my

men dispose of it?" Ben doesn't even spare a glance for Victor's dead body.

"I'll take him. I don't want to inconvenience you. But..." Artem looks with undisguised contempt at the man I shot.

They sound like they're discussing who will pay the bill. Very courteous.

"Not at all," Ben replies. "I'll handle that mess."

"Kind of you." Artem sucks his teeth. Victor is not a small man, but Artem sighs wearily, kneels and hefts his dead brother over his shoulder. "My thanks. Saved me a job. Come, Sergey. Fuck, I need a coffee," he mutters, then leaves.

"Thank you," Ben states. "For the tip-off."

It takes me a moment to realise he's talking to the youngest Bratva. Sergey.

Ohhh. Tom's boyfriend alerted Ben about my impending kidnap. I guess he didn't know that when that failed, his father would take Tom instead.

Sergey swallows and jerks a nod. "No problem." He transfers his gaze to Tom and I see adoration in his eyes. "I'll message you," stammers Sergey, and races away.

We're left, just the three of us.

"Dad." Tom doesn't move, and there's a new wariness on his face, different to the outright fear when he had a gun to his head.

"George, could you..." Ben waves at the dead goon on the floor.

George winks. "Got it, boss."

"Come." Ben wraps an arm around my waist and tows me out of the warehouse, Tom following. When we're safely ensconced in the limo Tom looks between Ben and me. We're not hiding. Ben has his hand on my shoulder, gently stroking me there. He kisses my head as soon as we are settled into seats, me next to Ben and Tom opposite.

Tension prickles up my bones as Tom takes in the casual intimacy.

"So... You two." He scowls.

"Yes," Ben replies simply, tilting up his chin as though to dare his son to say something.

"But... Anwyn?" Tom's lips press into a displeased line. "My ex-girlfriend? That's just... She's my age."

"A sexually mature adult, then," I point out.

Ben raises one eyebrow, a glint of amusement on his face. "The heart wants who it wants, Tom. Love isn't about age or nationality or... gender."

Tom digests that. "You knew."

"I've known you a long time," Ben replies.

"Right, but Anwyn." Tom rounds on me. "My dad? Couldn't you have—"

"You don't speak to her like that," Ben snaps. "And if we're talking about inappropriate choices of partner, we can start with the son of the mafia who has been attempting to take down Westminster for ten years."

Tom swears and drags both hands through his hair in a frustrated gesture so like Ben I have to laugh. "Are you going to ban me from being with him?"

Ben huffs out a breath that's equal parts irritation and amusement. "No. But I might use it to force you to accept Anwyn as your step-mum."

"No!" Tom looks so horrified.

"That's not how it will be," I cut in.

"Though you will have some half-siblings," Ben adds lazily. He's enjoying this and I shoot him a look. He gives me an unrepentant wink, mouths *breed you,* and I blush.

Tom winces. "Fine. If I can be with Sergey, fine. I never want to hear about any of how that happened. Ever."

Ben and I grin at each other. "Deal."

EPILOGUE
BENEDICT

10 years later

I still look forward to Saturdays. Particularly on drizzly winter late afternoon weekdays like this one, that has been a long sequence of minor mafia fracas to manage, followed by a report that I need to make a decision on. Westminster is more wealthy and powerful than ever, but there are always reasons for me to be wary, and keep looking out. Thankfully disputes with the Bratva are years in the past. But there's still a chunk of most of my days that requires me to work. Saturdays are a treat to look forward to because the Crosse family spends the whole day together.

Henry, our eldest son, is nine now. Serious and hardworking, Wyn says he's just like me. But his smile is identical to hers. Then there's Molly, seven, our tearaway. How Wyn and I produced a girl who loves to be naughty as much as she does, I don't know. Two years ago I found her sitting on the roof of Wyn's country house, calm as you like. I nearly had a heart attack. Elizabeth is four, and as sweet and funny as her mother.

Even Tom and his husband Sergey usually manage to come for lunch on Saturdays. Tom was a little freaked out when Wyn was pregnant, but Sergey—the sensible one of the two—took to the babies immediately and has become a sort of surrogate brother. I think his enthusiasm dragged Tom along, and I heard him broach the idea of starting their own family when Sergey was playing trains on the floor with Henry last month.

It's almost laughable how much work was my whole life, not so long ago. And there's still plenty to do. I tell myself it's a good thing, as Anwyn's job as a university professor is demanding, and the kids have to go to school. Even if I could pass off all responsibilities for Westminster, to spend all my time with my wife and kids I'd have to home educate our kids, and figure out ways to keep Anwyn entertained...

That doesn't sound terrible, actually.

Not yet. I love my kids and they deserve a better education than I'd provide. I turn my attention back to the report, my eye catching on a plant in my office that I'm sure wasn't there yesterday? I have so many now, and Wyn cares for them all, sneakily adding more, or swapping out ones that have finished flowering.

There's a tap on the door before it slowly opens and Henry peeks around the corner. "Dad?"

"Come in," I reassure him, turning off the screen to my computer. He might be born into the mafia, but that doesn't mean he'll see too much too young. I protect my family from the grittier aspects of my job. "Bring a chair."

He smiles and his bright blue eyes light up just as his mother's do. My heart melts a bit. Damn but I'm a fool for my kids.

"What is it?" I ask as he flops into the chair, having put it next to mine at the desk. I notice that he has an exercise book clutched in his hand.

"Science homework." I don't even have space to raise an eyebrow in surprise before he adds, "I know Mum is the one to ask about that, but she seemed really tired when she picked us up from school. I don't want to bother her."

I hide my smile. Tired, huh? I'd noticed the same and put it down to that time of the month, but if Henry has noted it too... Perhaps I should ask my wife a question this evening. There might be a moment for one of my favourite opportunities to look after her.

"Proud of you for being so considerate, Henry. You did the right thing." My boy can shoot five bullseyes in a row, but it's his emotional smarts that will get him to the top of whichever profession he chooses. I suspect it won't be the mafia. I have a fiver on Molly being more bloodthirsty and risk-taking than I am, and that she'll be my second-in-command by the time she's sixteen and running Westminster when I retire, though Wyn is convinced our middle child will end up in the circus.

"You're not as good at science as Mum, I know, but I thought maybe you could help me figure it out?" He holds out the exercise book, which has a sheet of paper with the printed homework slipped in.

I snort as I take it. Kids. Never going to hold back to save your pride, are they? I restrain myself from pointing out that I'm no slouch at chemistry (the bomb-making part of it, anyway), and physics (bullet trajectory is a specialist subject) and that his Mum is primarily good at biology (trees, and yes, she's an expert on making babies). Instead I say, "Sure, show me."

We work together for over an hour. After I've read the

assignment and explained it to him in a way he understands, he does the questions on his own, sitting at my desk
beside me while I read the report on a tablet. Angled away
from his curious eyes.

The scent of onions and garlic fried in oil wafting into
the room makes us look at each other. Thank god for Janet,
our housekeeper, who ensures everyone eats when Wyn
and I are distracted by work. Or each other—that's a thing
that happens too, just as often now as ten years ago when
Henry was conceived.

"Dinner," I tell Henry. "Go and set the table please, and
see if Janet needs any help with serving up please, and let
her know I'll be there in a minute with the girls."

Henry nods eagerly, always happy with a task and
responsibility and bounds away. I go to find Molly first.
She's playing a computer game that Wyn sometimes plays
with her. Zelda something, I think.

"Hey Dad." She doesn't look up from where she's
focussed on the blond boy–elf?—on screen. I wait a minute
while she tries to solve a puzzle, leaning over the back of her
sofa to watch my daughter. A couch in her room? I shake
my head internally. We really are indulgent parents.

She growls with frustration as she fails again.

I muss her hair as she pouts and tosses the controller
onto the cushion.

"Save it, and come and have dinner."

"Dad!" she whines.

"Molly!" I mimic back at her. "You'll figure it out better
with some brain food."

She huffs and follows me out. With her on her way to
the dining room, I head to the lounge where I suspect I'll
find my wife and youngest.

I do. In our jungle-like lounge, Elizabeth is watching a

cartoon, curled against Wyn who is leaned into the squashy sofa, asleep. There are work papers in her lap, and her blonde hair is spilt over her shoulders. She's wearing a cute knitted jumper and a pair of jeans and looks so adorable and good I want to hold her, unpeel her, and gobble her up like sweet apple pie.

Elizabeth's eyes light as I approach, reaching out her arms with a big smile, anticipating being picked up.

I nod. "Mummy first."

"Ben?" Wyn stirs as I kiss her forehead, but struggles to open her eyes.

"I think there's something you'll want to tell me, right?" I tease as I stroke her cheek. "It's okay. Stay here. I'll bring you some food in a bit."

"Mmm, 'anks," she slurs and flops deeper into the cushions. The first part of her pregnancy is always tiring. She needs her rest, and she knows I'll take care of everything. No need for her to get up if she needs to sleep.

I scoop Elizabeth into my arms. I'll have dinner with the kids and come and wake up my wife to eat later. And if she is pregnant again, as I suspect, I have the ideal way to make her comfortable.

I have just the idea to keep her warm and happy.

Fancy seeing what Ben does for Anwyn later that evening? (It's sexy!) Get the exclusive extended epilogue straight to your inbox.

Looking for more age gap romance with an obsessed stalker-ish kingpin hero? Check out *Owned by her Enemy*, with a mafia arranged marriage and heaps of sugar and spice.

EXTENDED EPILOGUE
ANWYN

10 years later, after dinner

"Time to eat, darling." My bossy husband appears in the doorway to the lounge.

I blink up at him as he comes to the side of the sofa where I've been napping—sorry I mean—watching television.

There's tenderness in his expression but also assessment as he looks at me, sprawled on the sofa. His gaze lingers on my midriff.

I yawn as I sit up. "Did I miss dinner again?"

He slides onto the sofa beside me, gorgeous as ever in a grey suit. His hair is more silver than it was when we met, but he's just as handsome. He passes over a bowl and spoon.

"Where are the kids?" I drag myself upright and the scent of food hits me. Yeah. I needed this. Even if I am tired enough to face-plant into it.

"In bed, or on their way. Janet is looking after everything."

"Thank you." I never have to ask him to help with the children, or anything like that. If I can't, he's on it immediately.

"No problem. Got something to tell me?" he drawls as I tuck into the rich spiced stew he brought, covered in cheese and topped with fresh herbs.

"Mmm." I avoid his eyes and pretend to chew.

"Are you going to be smuggling a watermelon soon?" he asks, voice warm with amusement.

That and busy barfing in the mornings and sleeping most of the day. I make a non-committal noise. He's so overprotective when I'm pregnant. I was hoping to have another week before he scowled at me for lifting so much as a mug.

"Tell me," he orders.

And oof. That tone. I put down my spoon and look up into his eyes. "You knocked me up. You know you did."

He grins—so pleased with himself he's well over the border into smug. "First time, right?"

"You're so arrogant," I mutter, but I'm grinning back at him. I lean into his reassuring bulk, shoulder to shoulder. He tells me in a soft voice about his day, and the kids, as I eat. Then takes the empty bowl from my hands and pulls me into his arms, and we sit together until I'm caught by a yawn, tiredness washing over me again.

"My girl," he murmurs. "I think you need to go to bed too, darling."

Then he gathers me up and lifts me, carrying me upstairs to our bedroom. The rest is soft-focus, as he undresses me with words of praise and touches to my body like he can't help himself. Like however tired I am, I'm still the energy he needs.

And when we snuggle into bed, he's the big spoon behind me, tucking me into his naked body.

"Do you want me inside you?" he asks into my ear, his breath soft.

I shiver with desire. "Yes."

He's so gentle and yet hard as a rock and fiery hot. The blunt tip of his cock presses into the gap between my thighs. He's hard, and I'm wet. It's always the way with us.

I know this will be different from when we're playing that he's creeping up on me at night and taking me against my will, or breeding me, or I'm a university student come to tempt him, or any of the games we indulge in. We started a slower type of sex when I was pregnant with Henry, and has become almost a treat and a tradition since.

"Shall I warm you up?" He grasps my top thigh and slides it over his, opening me up. He purrs as he feels my nod. "So wet for me. My good, good girl."

The push in is gradual, relishing our tight fit and I moan, tired as I am. I'm undeniably safe and loved. Ben's hand is plastered over the whole of my lower stomach, holding where my womb is just very slightly—or maybe it's my imagination—rounded with what will be our baby. And it's pushed out from him rearranging my insides. His other arm is over my chest and he's keeping me pressed to him. And he's so warm, everywhere.

"That's it," he whispers and pulls us closer, going deeper, then deeper still. He's big, and the first penetration is always tight. "You were made for me. Take it."

Shifting, he slides to the hilt, my butt squished onto his hips. The wetness spills out over my thighs, but it's toasty under the covers and it's all heat and comfort. While this morning when we had sex I came twice, I don't feel the need now.

This morning we were fucking. Coarse and hard and animalistic, we were ripping pleasure from each other, and tearing it from ourselves to give to the other. He growled about breeding me, and told me he'd fill me up with his seed.

Too late, ha. Already done that, to excellent effect. I swear Ben only has to fill me up once and I'm pregnant within five minutes.

But you don't have as much sex as we do and only three children—nearly four—in ten years without a lot of delicious pretence. Ben might tell me he's breeding me, but he knows about my birth control because we've discussed it at length. Admittedly, his eyes gleamed when I told him I wanted to try for another baby and when he came inside me later with a hoarse cry, that was a bit special.

Tonight, he's cockwarming. He's a heater element, and I'm his sheath. Instead of pounding into me, he remains motionless, soaking in my juices. The press of his hand on my abdomen makes him seem even bigger, stuffed full of my husband of almost ten years, each year sweeter and more fun than the last. And more tender.

He bred me, and now he's going to care for me.

His breath is warm on the back of my neck, and he lets out a contented sigh, gently kissing the lines between my hair and skin.

"I'm looking forward to seeing you pregnant again, Wyn. You're even more gorgeous with that curve." He rubs where I'll get swollen with his baby. He runs his hands over me with infinitesimal tenderness. No haste. He's warming me from the inside out. It's all unhurried and languorous, like we have a whole lifetime to tear at each other's clothes and crash into orgasms as well as enjoy each other's company. And love. I never doubt that Ben loves me. It's in his every touch, the changes he's made, the adaptations to our still-growing family. Even the way he enables me to continue my career rather than be solely his mafia queen.

My eyes close. So warm and snug, tired, and deliciously full. Ben is holding himself still inside of me, everlasting in his patience. His arms bracket me to him and the rough parts of his skin where he's scarred or covered with hair are made smooth being pressed to my back, no motion.

We breathe in unison. I'm happy and relaxed. He's my pacifier. With his hard cock inside me, there's no room for uncertainty—or anything but love and contentment. It's all just Ben, and the proof he loves and wants me.

Still. He wants me still after ten years together.

And it's that thought that's in my mind—our decade of happiness—as I drift off to sleep.

———

A tingle at my clit is the sensation I wake to, followed by the slick pressure on my insides. Ben, still rock solid between my legs and stuffed into me. He's behind me, in front, inside. His breath is on my head and his arms keep me safe.

It's dark when I open my eyes, but I'm refreshed. Invigorated, even though I think it's the middle of the night. I have no idea how long I slept.

I reach back and find his side, and he lets out a growling purr.

"How do you still have an erection, Ben?" I murmur teasingly.

"It's your fault," he whispers back. "You're too fucking sexy. If you weren't my fucking desirable wife, I would be able to sleep." He rolls his hips and it reveals I'm covered in cream for him.

"Was I out for long?"

"You needed to rest." This time it's a distinct thrust.

"Do you need to fuck?" I love him soaking in me, but this slow easing in and out might be even better. It's a gradually increasing tempo of mutual lust.

"Yes." Harder this time. "But also no. I need to make love to my sweet, pregnant wife." He bites my ear and I gasp.

"Yes."

"You *are* pregnant then." He eases out further and thrusts back deeper. "You're bred from me coming right by your womb, aren't you?"

I make a wordless sound of agreement and try to open myself up more, to get him deeper.

"My good girl got a baby fucked into her by her mafia kingpin husband." He finds one of my nipples with his hand and tweaks it cruelly. But the pleasure pain spikes right through me and my next moan is louder. He soothes the hurt and that feels even better as he rolls the sensitive point in his fingers.

"My pregnant whore," he whispers right in my ear, and the heat of shame combines with the warmth of affection at the love in his voice. "You're such a come slut."

Nodding, I dig my nails into his thigh, urging him on.

"You like it all over you, huh? You want to be over-flowing with seed?"

Sweat sticks to my skin as he accelerates and his other hand finds my clit, taking the cream from around where he's pistoning into me and spreading it up. Then he strokes mercilessly. He's deep and hard in me, and the combination of him caressing my clit from the outside too, and teasing my nipple, is overwhelming.

"Tell me how you love taking my cock," he demands. "Beg for my cock and your man's come."

"I love it. I want it," I beg.

"You were born to take all of me."

"Yes." It's a choked scream.

"Mine," he says and presses his teeth into my neck in a bite that shoves me right over the edge and into spasms of pleasure that sparkle behind my eyelids. Wave after wave hits me, each as wonderful as the last, seeming to exist in a gap of time that shouldn't exist, flowing through only us.

Then he's as incoherent as I am, growling about how beautiful I am, and how good I feel. How I take his cock perfectly, and I'm being a good girl for him. I lap up his praise as much as I get hot from the teasing degradation. Because I know, whatever he says, he loves me and is just as crazy for me as I am for him.

"Fuck, Anwyn." His grip on me tightens and his cock swells. "You are amazing. I'm going to fill up your pretty pussy with all the come you can take."

"Ben." I hold him to me as best I can.

"I love you," he groans as he shakes with his release.

"I love you too," I reply, and feel him shudder again as he hears my words. "Husband."

"Forever." He breathes in and kisses my hair as his trembling stops, gradually. "I won't let you go, Wyn."

I take his big sticky hand from between my legs and bring it to my lips. The scent of his come is mixed with my cream. As it always will be. "I'd never let you."

THANKS

Thank you for reading, I hope you enjoyed it.

Want to read a little more Happily Ever After? Click to get exclusive epilogues and free stories! or head to Evie-RoseAuthor.com

If you have a moment, I'd really appreciate a review wherever you like to talk about books. Reviews, however brief, help readers find stories they'll love.

Love to get the news first? Follow me on your favored social media platform - I love to chat to readers and you get all the latest gossip.

If the newsletter is too much like commitment, I recommend following me on BookBub, where you'll just get new release notifications and deals.

amazon.com/author/evierose

bookbub.com/authors/evie-rose

instagram.com/evieroseauthor

tiktok.com/@EvieRoseAuthor

INSTALOVE BY EVIE ROSE

Mafia Boss Marriage

Owned by her Enemy

I didn't expect the ruthless new kingpin—an older man, gorgeous and hard—to extract such a price for a ceasefire: a mafia arranged marriage.

Marrying the Boss

Baby Proposal

My boss walked in on me buying "magic juice" online... And now he's demanding to be my baby's daddy!

London Mafia Bosses

Captured by the Mafia Boss

I might be an innocent runaway, but I'm at my friend's funeral to avenge her murder by the mafia boss: King.

Taken by the Kingpin

Tall, dark, older and dangerous, I shouldn't want him.

I thought my mafia connections were in the past, and I was alone. But powerful mafia boss Sebastian Laurent hasn't forgotten me.

Stolen by the Mafia King

I didn't know he has been watching me all this time.

I had a plan to escape. Everything is going perfectly at my wedding rehearsal dinner until *he* turns up.

Caught by the Kingpin

The kingpin growls a warning that I shouldn't try his patience by attempting to escape.

There's no way I'm staying as his little prisoner.

Claimed by the Mobster

I'm in love with my ex-boyfriend's dad: a dangerous and powerful mafia boss twice my age.

Snatched by the Bratva

I have an excruciating crush on this man who comes into the coffee shop. Every day. He's older, gorgeous, perfectly dressed. He has a Russian accent and silver eyes.

Filthy Scottish Kingpins

Forbidden Appeal

He's older and rich, and my teenage crush re-surfaces as I beg the former kingpin to help me escape a mafia arranged marriage. He stares at me like I'm a temptress he wants to banish, but we're snowed in at his Scottish castle.

Captive Desires

I was sent to kill him, but he's captured me, and I'm at his mercy. He says he'll let me go if I beg him to take his...

CONTEMPORARY ROMANCE BY EVIE
ROSE WRITING AS EVE PENDLE

Secrets of Wildbrook

Her Nemesis until 5pm

He's grumpy, she's sunshine. Workplace rivals are about to get
snowed in together. And there's only one bed.

Her Fake Date Until Midnight

He's hot. Rich. Domineering. And grumpy.

She's kind, trapped, and soon to be broke.

Her Grumpy Neighbour until Halloween

He's gorgeous but grumpy

She's conspicuous, cheerful, and in a lot of trouble

Her Boss until Christmas

She can't stand him, but his offer is too tempting

He's a cynical billionaire with too many secrets

Printed in Great Britain
by Amazon

44717860R00067